SMUGGLER'S GUIDE

TALES FROM THE UNDERWORLD

MAZ KANATA

Being an Account of the Immutable Life and Outrageous Times of the Outer Rim's Infamous Crime Queen

From the relic-strewn battlefields of Ruusan to Takodana Castle, Maz Kanata has etched a deep mark in the crossroads of the underworld.

The legend of the Outer Rim's notorious pirate queen has waxed and waned through the centuries, and few eyewitnesses still live to testify to the events of their eras. Kanata did not suffer the existence of the slavers and spicers whose operations she upended. By robbing from the galaxy's filth, Kanata allowed those on the fringe to survive in defiance of the Galactic Republic's indifference.

From the seeds planted by Maz Kanata, the underworld branched out in contradictory complexity. Smuggling and black-market trading are two of the arts that lean toward a positive response to government rigidity. Slaving, extortion, and bloodsport are facets of the trade that can never be defended.

THIS SOUNDS MORE LIKE THE MAZ I KNOW.
—DEX

WHAT IS THE UNDERWORLD?

I have lived through many cycles. I have seen and achieved many things. I know this environment better than anyone, and things have changed in the last thousand years. Without exception, every newcomer to this shadow trade assumes that rules don't exist, and that they will enjoy limitless freedom in how they conduct business.

They quickly learn otherwise when they fail to walk away from their first transgression. For every realm has its masters; those ignorant of this power imbalance will forever remain thralls.

Criminal structures become calcified into hierarchies, thanks to high-turnover generations that chase immortality through tradition. The current underworld is dominated by five syndicates:

- **THE CRYMORAH.** Wild, amoral, and the least likely to be bound by unspoken ritual.

- **BLACK SUN.** Slavers and assassins with powerful friends among the Coruscant elite.

- **CRIMSON DAWN.** As of this turn, Crimson Dawn is the strongest syndicate. It enjoys a fragile alliance with the Pykes.

- **PYKE SYNDICATE.** The Pykes control Kessel and therefore the Spice Triangle. They have muscled their way into Hutt circles and show no signs of slowing.

- **THE HUTTS.** The only underworld power that has stood since antiquity. Their complacency has allowed the Pykes (and a sixth syndicate, Son-Tuul Pride) to gain reputation at their expense.

To make a living in the shadow trade, many players take up temporary or bonded allegiance to one of the syndicates. The rest must gather enough scraps to survive as an independent.

Wherever governments cannot enforce the law, the syndicates thrive through simple intimidation: *Pay or we kill you.* These threats work on the powerless, providing the extortion income that keeps many crime organizations afloat. Few kingpins wish to start a gang war, and thus the underworld inevitably settles into an uneasy peace defined by hierarchies and turf.

LEADING SYNDICATES

(AS WELL AS MANY LESSER SYNDICATES, CARTELS, GUILDS, AND GANGS)

Richer than the Emperor himself, and not worth a bucket of reek sweat. —Han

CRIMELORDS

RUN THE SYNDICATES.

VIGOS AND UNDERBOSSES

MAKE ALLIANCES AND ORDER EXECUTIONS.

LIEUTENANTS

RUN SPECIFIC TERRITORIES.

Beneath these are the myriad ranks of those
who find work in the underworld.

- Smugglers, gunrunners, bootleggers, hunt spoilers, hazmat dumpers
- Kidnappers, thieves, extortionists, blackmailers
- Legbreakers, bodyguards, mercenaries, poachers
- Outlaw techs, ship modders, cyborg docs   *Cloners? Cryptosurgeons? —Dr. Evazan*
- Counterfeiters, embezzlers, credit launderers, usurers,
  black marketers, criminal fences
- Gamblers, bookmakers, fight fixers, *and irresistible gentlemen*
                                                          —Lando
- Saboteurs, arsonists
- Pirates, shipjackers, bandits, gunslingers

Criminal organizations enjoy symbiotic relationships with nearly every legitimate institution, including law enforcement, judicial departments, government legislators, and the military.

I block the worst syndicate trash from my castle. They always pay their tab, but too often their visits end with bodies that need cleaning up. There's a reason why I built this castle on a world next to a hyperspace nexus.

The outcasts always find their way here. I see every face that passes through my door. They are the pied patchworks that add color to a black-and-white galaxy.

While I have watched the underworld shift and shape itself time and again, I have learned the many secrets. Some do not believe the lore that has drifted across the tables and over drinks. I hear it again and again: "Maz, if you were a pirate queen, where'd it all go?" I tell them about relatable setbacks they're eager to believe. But the truth is that my reign netted me a lot more than a basement of antiques. *Aye, I know the feeling well. ~Gunda Mabin*

Each of the sites marked on this map contains a buried vault armed with an antitamper subspace alarm. To date, no such alarm has ever sounded.

The full scope of what I have to reveal will not fit into this log. This is why I have stashed high-density datalogs within forgotten storage nodes. To retrieve them, one must slice these location coordinates:

Q5T8L3BLT99MZX

7W9DMWVFG46USQ

VQZMBG8K6BSQA8

PCT2QV24932XPA

Intriguing. A polyniqmic cipher, I presume. —Master Codebreaker

YLGJDPVFDTA69L

L8ET35QRF7PNMD

ER28WZALGD8TPD

ZC8B7PEPP46KK9

As I prepare to add more words to this log, I see how this recording could shape destinies and influence fates. In times yet to come, the galaxy will be fundamentally remade. This book may pass between light and shadow, between the just and beasts alike. Its journey is one I must start.

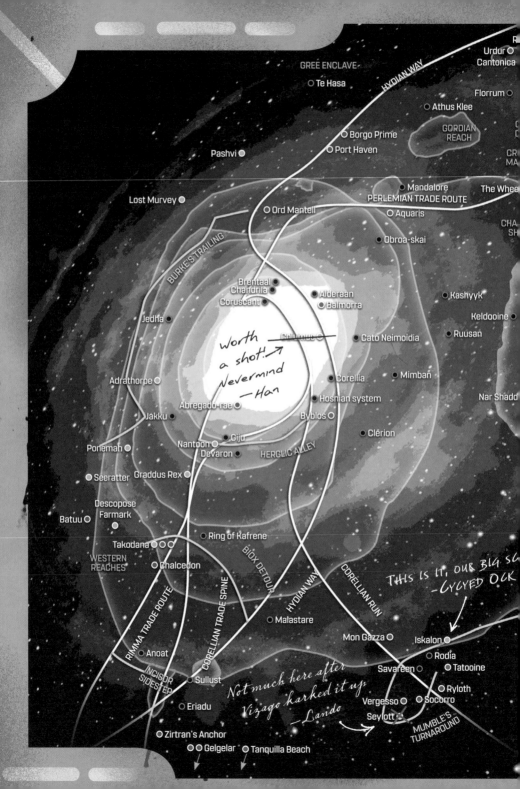

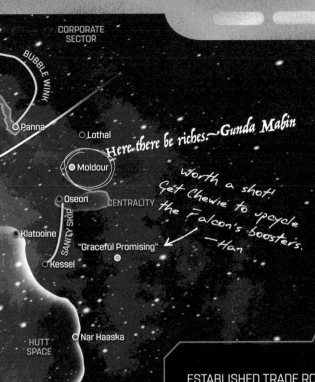

CORPORATE
SECTOR

BUBBLE WINK

○ Panna

○ Lothal

Here there be riches.—Gunda Mabin

● Moldour

○ Oseon

CENTRALITY

*Worth a shot!
Get Chewie to upcycle
the Falcon's boosters.
—Han*

SANITY SKIP

● Klatooine

"Graceful Promising" ●

○ Kessel

HUTT
SPACE

○ Nar Haaska

○ Ylesia

LEGEND

ESTABLISHED TRADE ROUTES:

THE REAL TRADE ROUTES:

- ● SHADOWPORTS
- ● OUTLAW GARAGES
- ● TREASURE CACHES
- ○ LOCATIONS OF INTEREST

SMUGGLING CARGOES THAT OFFER THE
MOST PROFIT PER KILOGRAM:
- Coaxium (timely delivery is critical)
- Quarren artisanal ink
  (used in Hutt kajidic tattoos)
- Harch industrial adhesive
- Gaberwool flaxen fibers
- Kibnon or Nevoota stimulant pollen
- Megonite moss (stable packaging is critical)

Starting today, everything turns around for Tryphon Leo.

Trade routes, shadowports, criminal contacts, hidden treasures—it's all in here, exactly as I suspected.

A single one of those treasures will set me up with enough credits to buy my own fleet of cratehaulers. Once I get my smuggling network running, I can nab the rest of the treasures and become richer than Xim. I am going to squeeze the galaxy's hyperlanes of every drop of wealth, and all I had to do to achieve it was flirt with that dried-up orange fossil.

Oh sure, I'd heard the stories: "Maz likes the bold ones." Or Maz likes the bashful ones, or the hairy ones, or the scaly ones, or the soft ones, or the hard ones. Maz likes everyone and no one, and it all comes down to what she thinks she "sees."

I knew it couldn't be that hard, and so I made myself a regular at her castle. I traded favors with the bartenders and slipped credits to the kitchen staff. I made that whole place love me, until finally the great Maz Kanata just had to check me out for herself. She's more quirky than all-knowing, as if the last of her entry isn't proof enough.

She sat across from me at that table all stony, not even touching the drink I'd bought for her. But then she slid down those macrospecs to squint at me, taking in my good looks with her beady eyes.

I knew I had her when she readjusted her specs and said, "You'll do."

I'm not some green-eared novice. I've put in my time. I've earned the right to use this info and to shake up the underworld.

As a freelancer, I smuggled everything from blasters to body parts—half payment upfront and no questions asked. As a spice runner, I've scraped the *Lessu Dancer*'s hull on carbonbergs while threading the Corkscrew. I've got memberships in the Corellian Merchants' Guild and the Mandroxan Cartel both.

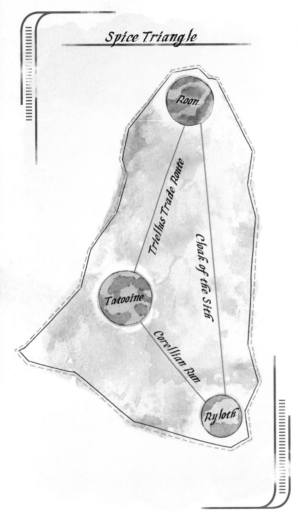

Spice Triangle

Roon

Triellus Trade Route

Cloak of the Sith

Tatooine

Corellian Run

Ryloth

NEW TRADE NETWORK:
Tryphon Leo's toll routes

So I'm thinking that once I purchase a fleet (maybe twenty HWK-290s, fifty YT-freighters, one hundred barges), I'll lock down trade along the Spice Triangle.

All smuggling along the Death Wind Corridor will go through me, plus I'll collect fees from the most lucrative segments of the Triellus and the Corellian Run.

I'll need to pay off the Hutts and the Pykes, at least at first, and the Imperial governor of Roon too. But who doesn't take bribes this far from the Core?

Today, I looked up an outfitter on Vergesso, a place that Maz recommended. Spent most of my savings on gear, but in a week, I'll have the money to buy this whole asteroid.

Decided I'm going to hit the treasure on Pashvi first. It isn't far, not at the speeds the *Lessu Dancer* can hit. And I can load the whole treasure myself using just a gravsled. No need to split it with a partner when I can take a 100 percent cut.

Crimson Dawn flexes its muscles in this part of space, so I'm keeping quiet. Not a peep to the natives about the destination I decoded from Maz's coordinates: the Shrove of the Left-Handed God Typhojem.

Yes, things are going to be different from now on for Tryphon Leo—the richest man who ever lived!

You said it, Chewie. Some people are dead set on getting themselves killed. —Han

LEAGUE OF XENOEXPLORERS

MEMBER NAME:
Reginald Danfillo

MEMBER RANK:
Senior terrain trekker, silver leaf, fullbloom cluster

I recovered this item at the site of the Typhojem Excavation. During the same outing, I collected Quesoth pottery shards and a piece of tapestry dating to the Neo-Middle Secundus. So imagine my disappointment that this thing is CONTEMPORARY and not a relic at all.

Item was discovered approximately seventy meters along the Grand Causeway, adjacent to a massive stone block presumably dislodged from the ceiling. Previous owner was human, probably, based on analysis of hand and forearm extending from beneath the block [see attachment].

Maybe spacer trash will pay for this. Looks like their kind of thing.

Note the Typhojem Thrall on the far wall.
— Reginald

WELL WHAT DO YOU KNOW! MAZ KANATA.

THAT DOES ME GOOD, SEEING THAT NAME AGAIN. WASN'T SO LONG AGO THAT I CALLED MYSELF HER BOYFRIEND. FOUR-ARMED MASSAGE WAS MY SPECIALTY! I'VE STILL GOT HER LETTERS INSIDE AN OLD AMMO BOX. DEXI JET IS WHAT SHE CALLED ME. STILL WARMS MY HEART. *And people say I'm charming.*
—Lando

AH, WHO AM I KIDDING. IT WAS LONG AGO. WHEN YOU GET AS OLD AS ME THE YEARS SEEM LIKE THEY'RE NOT WORTH SO MUCH. MEMORIES EITHER FEEL LIKE A CENTURY AGO OR YESTERDAY, NO IN BETWEEN.

I FOUND THIS LOGBOOK IN A BOX OF READING MATERIAL, TUCKED BETWEEN *THE BIOGRAPHY OF MASTER THIEF MAKUTA* AND *THE FIELD GUIDE TO TRAMMIC REPTAVIANS.* MAZ KANATA'S NAME ON THE FIRST PAGE DREW ME IN, AND THAT'S WHY MY POCKETBOOK IS FIFTY CREDITS LIGHTER.

A YOUNGER BESALISK MIGHT GO AFTER THE TREASURES, BUT JUST KEEPING HER NAME CLOSE IS GOOD ENOUGH FOR ME.

SINCE I WROTE THE ABOVE I'VE DITCHED PASHVI AND BOOKED PASSAGE FOR THE STELLAR SKIRT OF THE TINGEL ARM. HEARD ABOUT STRANGE THINGS OUT THERE: ILLEGAL CYBORG MODS AND BODIES GROWN TO FIT BUYER SPECS, TO NAME JUST TWO.

CLONERS, MAYBE, PLYING THEIR TRADE FOR PRIVATE CLIENTS? THERE'S PLENTY OF WORK OUT THERE FOR THOSE TYPES, NOW THAT THE SYNDICATES CONTROL THE OUTER RIM.

THE STAR-STEAMER MADE PORT ON ATHUS KLEE THIS MORNING. THE PASSENGERS POURED OUT AND MELTED INTO THE SPACERS' DISTRICT, BUT ME, I DON'T MOVE AS FAST AS I USED TO. BY THE TIME I MADE IT DOWN THE RAMP EVERY SINGLE INN HAD NO ROOMS.

SO I WALKED OUT INTO THE UNDERBRUSH AND FOUND A RISE THAT WASN'T TOO DAMP, AND THEN I SPLAYED OUT UNDER THE STARS.

I CAN'T BLAME ALL THOSE HOPEFULS FOR HEADING OUT THIS WAY. CRIMSON DAWN POSTED BIG-MONEY CONTRACTS FOR LABORERS. "ONE YEAR," THEY ALL THINK, "I CAN MAKE IT ONE YEAR." MOST OF THEM WILL BE DEAD BEFORE THEN.

MY FAVORITE PART OF TRAVELING IS HOW THE SKY ALWAYS HAS NEW STARS. I GUESS SOME OF THEM ARE PROBABLY THE SAME STARS, BUT EVERYTHING LOOKS DIFFERENT FROM A NEW ANGLE.

FOUR DAYS INTO THE JUNGLE NOW. PLENTY GLAD I BROUGHT THAT VIBRO-MACHETE.

I'M CLOSE TO WHAT I CAME HERE FOR. I CAN FEEL IT IN MY GUT. AND WHO COULD ARGUE WITH A GUT LIKE THIS?

SIX DAYS, TWO VIPER BITES, AND MORE GNAT NIPS THAN I CAN COUNT. BUT SURE AS YOU'RE BORN, THAT'S A CRIMSON DAWN ORE HUB DOWN IN THAT VALLEY.

ROCK HAULERS HEADING OUT AND PASSENGER SHUTTLES HEADING IN WITH MORE WORKERS TO FEED THE MACHINE.

HAD TO DO SOME SNEAKING, BUT ON THE FAR SIDE OF THE PROCESSING PLANT, I FOUND A CLUSTER OF HEXAGONAL SILOS, LIKE A HIVE. THAT'S A GENE-MOD CHOP SHOP.

I RECORDED SOME MACROBINOCULAR SCANS. POOR BASTARDS. HANDS TURNED INTO SHOVEL BLADES. NOSES AND MOUTHS SWITCHED OUT WITH BIOMESH FOR FILTERING TOXINS. EYES BIG AS PLATES TO COLLECT THE LIGHT THAT MAKES IT ALL THE WAY DOWN TO THE DEPTHS.

Not my best work. I confess. But why waste my genius on syndicate moneymen?
—Dr. Evazan

RECORDING // 40X ZOOM

13

EVEN THE KAMINOANS HAD SOME PRIDE IN THEIR WORK, BUT CRIMSON DAWN ONLY WANTS TO BUILD MORE EFFICIENT MINERS AND THEN WORK 'EM TILL THEY'RE DEAD. FATES ONLY KNOW WHAT KIND OF BUTCHER THEY'VE GOT ON THEIR PAYROLL.

I CAN'T SAVE THEM ALL. I'M JUST ONE PERSON. I CAN'T EVEN SAVE ONE OF THEM.

OKAY, OKAY, MAZ WAS RIGHT. I'M SOFT IN THE HEAD. I'M HEADING BACK TO THE STARPORT WITH MY RECORDINGS, BUT THIS TIME I'M BRINGING A BUDDY.

HE CAN'T TALK—AT LEAST NOT CLEAR ENOUGH FOR ME TO UNDERSTAND—BUT HE KNOWS WHAT HAPPENED TO HIM JUST THE SAME. I KNOW STEALING ONE WORKER WON'T MAKE ANY DIFFERENCE TO CRIMSON DAWN. BUT I FIGURED IT'D MAKE A DIFFERENCE TO THIS GUY.

LAST NIGHT WE JUST LAY ON OUR BACKS FOR HOURS, STARING UP THROUGH A BREAK IN THE CANOPY. HE LIKES THE STARS.

MADE IT TO THE PORT THIS MORNING AND COMMED MY BUDDY ON CORUSCANT. AS POLITICIANS GO HE'S ONE OF THE GOOD ONES. HE'S SENDING A SHIP TO COLLECT MY NEW PAL ALONG WITH MY SURVEILLANCE DATA, THEN TAKING EVERYTHING BEFORE THE SENATE COUNCIL OF LABOR ABUSES.

I'M NOT SO RAW TO THINK THIS'LL SHUT DOWN THE SYNDICATES OR ANYTHING—NOT WHEN THEY'RE THE CLOSEST THING SOME SECTORS HAVE TO A FUNCTIONING GOVERNMENT. BUT IT MIGHT PUT A STOP TO THOSE LABORATORY HORROR SHOWS, AND THAT MAKES TODAY A PRETTY GOOD DAY.

This is ringing a bell. Should probably show it to—Nah. She doesn't want to talk to me. —Han

Tyro Viveca

That is enough of all that. Besalisks have the wits of children. I can only assume that moving four arms requires their spongy brains to work double time!

The specimen, Dexter Jettster, I shared a drink with inside the Rasher's Rest was no exception. I can only hope he learned a lesson about leaving his belongings unattended while visiting the latrine.

This book he possessed intrigued me. I filled the last page of my Vandor field journal only yesterday, so this will do as a replacement.

Let me start a fresh page.

Tyro Viveca

Xenonaturalist, Bagger of Rare Animals, Preserver of Hunting Grounds, Tamer of Predators, and Lover of Wildlife

ENTRY 1

As I deepen my fame and enrich my fortune, my perilous trek has brought me from the wilds of Athus Klee to the blackest depths of Kashyyyk. Here I shall track the elusive beast of legend and lore that has tantalized naturalists for generations: the terentatek.

But no longer! This safari shall see Tyro Viveca bag a full-sized specimen for taxidermy preservation. Barring that, the head will do, mounted on a plaque inscribed with my name and the gauge of the weapon used to bring down the beast.

MY QUARRY

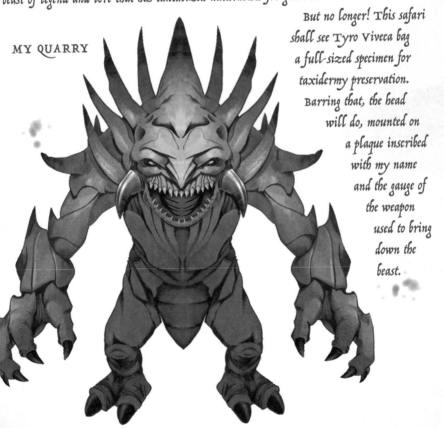

THE TERENTATEK IN THE STANCE I PREFER FOR TAXIDERMY. PERHAPS WITH THE RAISED CLAWS.

ENTRY 2

I booked passage aboard an Ugor steamer on its way to the Wookiee world. It is a challenge to tolerate the stink emanating from these shapeless jelly bags. Hardly any room for a brain inside that oozing mess!

Three days in this hotbox already. Speaking very slowly and at great volume so that the captain might comprehend, I asked when the ship would make port at Kashyyyk. The thing pecked at my datapad with a foul pseudopod, spelling the word "SOON."

It had better be. I hunger to partake in the noblest of sports, and my patience is running out.

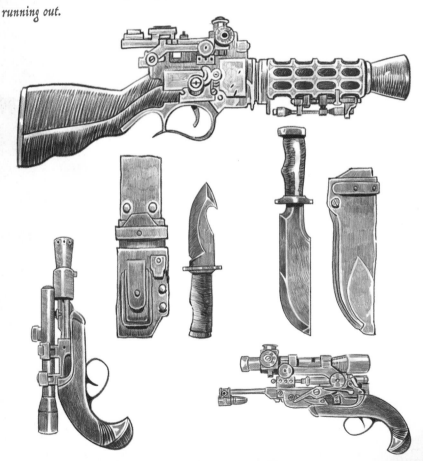

ENTRY 3

Today I stood on soil once more, by which I mean the tarmac of the Thikkiiana spaceport on Kashyyyk.

The rule of the Emperor suits a rough place like this. The port is clean and efficient, and the Republic's antipoaching statutes have been voided planetwide. Hurrah for the Emperor, I say! Let wildlife be wild.

ENTRY 4

Ten kilometers beyond the tree line I have already met kindred spirits. At this seasonal encampment Trandoshans stage hunts for Wookiee pelts and scalps. A fine game indeed!

After comparing weapons—my Drearian against the huntmaster's Tenloss—we swapped tales by the firelight. I learned that a previous party of Trandoshans, eager for distraction, had excavated a hole and ringed it with sharpened stakes. At my

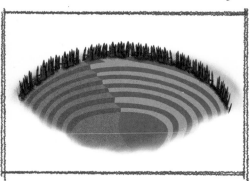

THE MAKESHIFT ARENA

urging, the Trandoshans emptied cages into the pit, releasing two frenzied animals.

The maddened beasts set upon each other: the first, a serpentine crawler with dripping pincers; the other, a bristled prowler with short claws and amusingly oversized ears.

What a grand diversion! To a man, we placed our bets, and I won the prize by predicting the prowler's demise within two minutes. I am one who has seen bursa-baiting on Ohma-D'un and monster fights on Geonosis, and a true sportsman can always recognize the killer instinct.

THREE CHEERS FOR BLOODSPORT!

Agreed! Ponda. I have found a kindred spirit.
— Dr. Evazan

ENTRY 5

The Trandoshans are far behind me now. Still no sign of the terentatek.

Before making camp, I incinerated a nest of juvenile sureggi so their mother would not view me as a threat to her nestlings. No nestlings, no threat. The simple mind of the animal!

ENTRY 6

Terentatek spoor found in the lower tiers of the jungle canopy. Sunlight does not penetrate this deeply, but luminous fungus is sufficient to light my way.

This terentatek is crafty, but it has never faced a sportsman such as myself. It will all be over soon.

W ell now, what befell this poor man? Who can say? His fate is his own concern, so long as he does not come looking for his log. I tell you, not everyone knows that the city of Thikkiiana has a lost-items office! Every time I pass this way, I visit there during the dusk shift and I say, "It is I, Hondo Ohnaka." And the desk clerk, so lovely and unappreciated, will let me leave there with a hovertank.

A logbook is no hovertank, but I left with this one all the same. What to do with it? I wonder.

My sweet mother always said, "Son, grab everything you can, but if you don't use it, why bother?" And a flip through these pages just now gives me a good feeling for profit yet to come. For even the great Hondo Ohnaka recognizes the value of the name Maz Kanata. Buried treasure and great secrets—many will pay for knowledge such as this.

Could this book be false, made to separate the fool from his credits? I think no, but the idea of it is inspiring a new business plan.

"What is an item worth? Whatever the buyer thinks it is worth." My mother, bless her horns. I see riches falling from the sky!

|||||||||||||||||||||||||||||||||||||||||||||||||||||||||||||||||||||||||||||||||||||||||||||||||||||||||||||||||||

It is as my mother always said, "Luck visits the prepared." And so I am back on Florrum, where the dregs of the Ohnaka gang cling to the bottom of a bottle.

What times we all had, back in the Clone Wars! In those days, upheaval meant opportunity. I commanded a great empire and even held Count Dooku as a hostage! Was a ransom of 1,000,000 credits asking too much? I only dream big dreams!

Here on Florrum is where I will find my master forger, Bar the Rotter, in the Cellar of Penitence at the Church of Infinite Perception. The criminal life inspires self-reflection for some, especially in the later years. How fortunate that I do not suffer from the same affliction!

PROPERTY OF:
Hondo Ohnaka

Bar the Rotter hard at work on a master copy or
reflecting on life—one is never too sure these days.
— Hondo Ohnaka

21

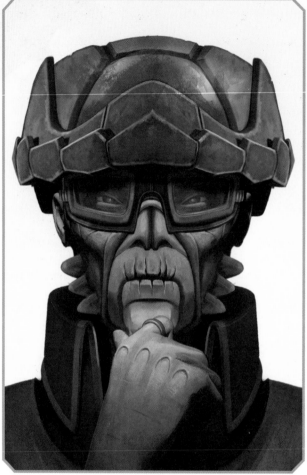

The teachings of my loving mother, so warm and profitable, have never steered me astray. It seems to me that others may benefit from Hondo Ohnaka's example should I collect these observations into a book and price that book accordingly.

Possible book titles?

The Ohnaka Codex

The Book of Hondo

Weequay Wisdom and Assorted Aphorisms, compiled by Captain Hondo Ohnaka

Words have value, do they not? What is their market rate?

Just don't go stepping on The Calrissian Chronicle. —Lando

I leave Florrum with another victory. Hondo Ohnaka's triumph continues apace!

Bar the Rotter had no wish to abandon his order—not for credits, or women, or fame. Drink? That was another matter.

> ## "EVERYTHING IS FOR SALE, AND NOT ALWAYS FOR MONEY."
> *—THE BOOK OF HONDO*

I am with my dear friend Bar the Rotter, and we are already halfway to Balmorra.

He has not forged a document in years, but today he tried his hand at reproducing the script in this very journal. Right now he sleeps, sprawled on the cabin floor and making sounds with his mouth that I cannot describe.

The Whyren's Reserve I have on board is the only thing that quells his tremors. Sleep well, my friend, and may these bottles never run dry.

> **"FOOD, DRINK, AND THE COMPANY OF OTHERS: CREDITS CAN BUY ALL THREE."**
> *—THE BOOK OF HONDO*

Ah, Balmorra. It is an ugly place coated in a sticky film. Yet here I will find the Marquess. You see, I am in need of someone to manipulate the Undervine network, a job I suspect will require the subtle touch of one particular woman.

If it all goes according to plan, and why should it not, Bar the Rotter will complete three logbook forgeries. The Marquess will reach out to buyers on the anonymous Undervine and arrange for three auctions. The bidders will not know of the competing auctions until long after credits have changed hands.

!!

In Balmorra's Swellbottom market I found one of the stores that sells animals for credits.

No creature in there impressed me, and they had one Kowakian monkey-lizard only. I did not buy it, for I did not like the way it looked at me.

> ## "NEVER TRUST ANYONE MORE CHARMING THAN YOURSELF."
> *—THE BOOK OF HONDO*

The Marquess, she was not happy to see me! Imagine such a thing if you can. She, employed as a numerical actuary, and I, Hondo Ohnaka, bearing a guarantee of adventure. My handsomeness, this is also something she should have taken into account!

Alas, the Marquess has grown too dull to see my charms. She joined my crew, but only after negotiating for a cut of 30 percent. No matter. Wealth will be had by all!

> ## "ONLY A FOOL TAKES THE FIRST OFFER."
> *—THE BOOK OF HONDO*

Today the Marquess baited the lure. The first auction of *Maz Kanata's Journal* (complete with certificate of authenticity) will take place in the panopticon garret above the casino floor on Zirtran's Anchor.

This chamber is surely the most closely surveilled room in the entirety of the Phosphura Belt. Who could pull a double cross in such a place?

Bidding starts at 75,000 credits, since I already had to pay 5,000 credits just to rent the room.

> ## "APPEARANCES ARE NINE-TENTHS OF THE TRUTH, AND CHARM CAN COVER THE REST."
> *—THE BOOK OF HONDO*

The ship is docked, the room is ready. At 1630, the auction begins. It ends at 1730 when our reservation expires.

Attending are agents from the Rang Clan, the Xrexus Cartel, and Novabarrel Distillery (a front company for the Hutts).

Bar the Rotter will play the part of rare document expert. The Marquess will make a convincing security guard.

As for refreshments, I had six bottles of Whyren's Reserve before Bar found the storeroom key. Now half a bottle remains. But small portions, this is a sign of refinement!

Once the auction concludes and the credits are transferred, we jump for the next auction in the Boro-borosa system.

> ## "STAY NIMBLE, FOR SPEED CAN OUTRUN SUSPICION."
> *—THE BOOK OF HONDO*

ATTENTION CON ARTISTS: SOME OF US CAN SPOT FAKE RELICS ON SIGHT. THIS XENOARCHAEOLOGY DEGREE ISN'T JUST FOR SHOW.
—APHRA

Before blame is assigned, I wish to point out that I could not have known that the Rang Clan would bring a document authenticator. Nor could I have foreseen that Bar the Rotter would spell so many words so poorly! Including "Maz Kanata" apparently! You ask too much of Hondo Ohnaka, imaginary interrogator.

It is good that I had prepared for such a catastrophe. At the first sign of a blaster, the Marquess jerked her neck to rattle the gears inside her headpiece. Every screen on the walls flashed white at the same time, blinding anyone who hadn't closed their eyes. How unfortunate then that the Xrexus Cartel had brought a droideka.

We hastened for the turbolift, but the thing rolled down the corridor and unfolded into attack stance, close enough for me to sniff the ozone from its charged-up cannons.

Naturally, I closed the turbolift doors as soon as I had slipped inside. Should I have held them open for the others? Who would benefit should I perish?

> ### "BE LOYAL TO YOUR PARTNERS, UNTIL BETTER PARTNERS COME ALONG."
> *—THE BOOK OF HONDO*

And also, it was not very big in there, my friend. Perhaps not big enough for three to fit comfortably! Blame the designer of that turbolift.

Suddenly I'm glad I turned down Hondo's shaak-breeding scam in the Cron Drift. —Lando

As I feared, word has spread on the Undervine about the forgery. This line of work is no longer profitable. Hondo Ohnaka must seek a new fortune, and with haste.

> ### "TEN CREDITS TODAY BEATS 100 CREDITS TOMORROW."
> *—THE BOOK OF HONDO*

Among Bar the Rotter's belongings I found a polished stone that he used for meditating on his church's teachings. I obtained a similar state of enlightenment when I took the stone with me to the Kafrene bordellos. It was there that I foresaw that Hondo Ohnaka would become . . . a pirate! Once again!

I have my ship; I need only a crew. Who would pass up the chance to win such glory? It is now clear to me that obtaining a monkey-lizard is essential, for I must look the part.

Clear skies and good business are out there, and they await Hondo Ohnaka!

> ### "THERE'S ALWAYS ANOTHER ANGLE."
> *—THE BOOK OF HONDO*

"Y OU HAVE AN EYE FOR TREASURE, GUNDA, yet have no stomach for slaughter." These words Captain Carabba laid upon my ears every day, beginning when I was a wee cabin cub and long after I took over as mate. He was still talking when I stilled his lips forever with a blade to his ribs. No stomach for slaughter? His insides on the deck said otherwise.

Yet Carabba was true about the other—an eye for treasure I have. That is why I plucked this logbook from out of the haul we took from that mynock-scraper, Hondo Ohnaka. He is one that only plays at pirate. He knows better than to tangle with the real thing.

Being an account of the plunder seized from that snakebit cur, Hondo Ohnaka

Coaxium, 32.5 units
Onyx pearls, 0.80 kg
Serrated vibroblade
DX-13 blaster pistol
Elixir of Omwat's Grace
Fine oro-weave vest trimmed with nerfwool
Rhen-Orm biocomputer module
chromium hand mirror
Whyren's Reserve, sixteenth
vintage (half bottle)

I spared Ohnaka from the void. Better he be a living warning to all those who ply the spacelanes: beware the Blazing Claw, and beware Gunda Mabin–captain of the *Bloody Bones* and master of a hundred ships more!

'Tis a curious thing, this collection. I care not for the prattles of Ohnaka, and still less for anything written by dirt treaders. Yet the name at the start of it all stunned me square. The pirate queen of yore: Kanata the Despoiler, Kanata the Benevolent. She who held sway over a thousand ports when the Republic was new.

With my enemies, I can never cross her Takodana doorstep, not if I wish to leave again. But by the seven fiends–here in my hands is something better. Kanata of the Free Fleet speaks to me from across the seas of centuries.

Our course is decided. All crew shall assemble. On this eve, we set a course for the treasure of Maz Kanata!

FIFTH SIDEREAL CYCLE THE TWENTY-THIRD

Have I not earned the right to claim these riches? Indeed I have, since the day I donned Carabba's black cap.

We sail for the moons of Moldour, while other ships of my fleet have orders to harry merchants along the outer Hydian and as far as the spillways of Ashcan Reach. 'Tis better to keep the Empire looking elsewhere so its agents don't cast their eyes on the *Bloody Bones*. And should we also hoodwink the Dharus Buccaneers, all for the good! I will not be sharing treasure with those fever rats.

FIFTH SIDEREAL CYCLE THE THIRTY-FIRST

Twelve hours ago, Punter roused me from where I was sleeping. He kept needling "Captain!" in his rotten Chadra chitters, causing Rosallia to squawk dismally from her perch.

The *Bloody Bones* had sprung a leak. We'd been spilling coaxium since the Port of Ottega. Unless I took action, my proud ship would lay cold among the stars before the next shift turn.

Pirate can't evolve from the pidgin tongues of ancient Paecia. Have entered this into my calculations.—Master Codebreaker

I took the helm and under my hand, the *Bloody Bones* washed out of hyperspace into the busiest stretch of the Atrian Merchants' Causeway. Our gauges burned red. Punter was in a panic, eyeing the rate of coaxium bleed. I steered the ship strong and true, bearing down on a Ghtroc star yacht that would never again see the pleasures of port.

"Flash the colors and ready to fire!" I cried. The holocam summoned a ghostly Blazing Claw, matching the ones emblazoned on our bow and stern.

The *Bloody Bones* fired a broadside shot. Our fusillade splashed across the enemy's shields, splintering them in places. I brought the *Bloody Bones* alongside as Hawson threw open the starboard hatch. Using his droid arm, Handsome Tar tossed magnesium burners through the magnetic field that fixed tight against the yacht's hull, marking a two-meter circle. I narrowed my eyes as the flares ignited. One shot from a powder kicker knocked that piece of hull inward, and our boarding party followed close behind.

After a time, the yacht's transponder switched over to Zeta Zeta Zeta, Hawser's sign that the fighting was over. White clouds from flash bombs lingered in the air. A few of the yacht's rashest crewmembers lay in pieces, neatly cleaved by Grullbug's hand. With the ship in such a sorry state, I hardly needed to pluck the vial from my pocket and light the quickfire that sheathed my tusks in green flame, but a canny pirate queen must sustain her infamy.

The yacht's captain begged for his life, earning him a trip out the airlock. The others hastily surrendered the lockcodes for the ship's coaxium.

Now they await salvation aboard a darkened and silent vessel, dwelling upon their encounter with Gunda Mabin and her infamous pirates. And so my legend grows.

FIFTH SIDEREAL CYCLE THE THIRTY-THIRD

The *Bloody Bones* is again hale and hearty. My ship feasts on coaxium, and a welded deck plate is a fine reactor patch. 'Twas a sorry end for Punter, buckling under the radiation while finishing the job. Mayhap he should have refrained from waking his captain as she slept off the prior night's revels.

FIFTH SIDEREAL CYCLE THE THIRTY-FIFTH

From the helm, navigator Puckwale reports that we shall reach Moldour 14 in the morning. Then the treasure of Maz Kanata will be mine.

I will outstrip her legacy. I will forever be the Pirate Queen of the Outer Rim.

FIFTH SIDEREAL CYCLE THE THIRTY-SIXTH

I should have suspected that others would see the value of this log, and would also know that I would never surrender it if my body still held breath. The instant I slipped the *Bloody Bones* into a Moldour orbit, Patchwork Fiddich pulled a pistol from his coat.

"We thank you for the ride, Captain." Did he honestly think I would stand to be his shuttle service, that I would back down that easy? That *he* claim that treasure! He be the captain of my ship! A crew is only as strong as it is disposable. Six of my crew stood with him, and the others made nary a move. In that moment, I knew that Fiddich had lost this gamble.

I took one step forward. Fiddich instinctively took a step back. His face bore the scars of the Burning, back when Carabba had shoved his cheek against a blaster's muzzle and peeled skin from flesh. I could see in his gaze that he would forever fear true power. Yet he steeled his spine and planted his feet. We stared at each other as my tongue quested in my mouth for my false grinder. I bit down hard on the glass tooth. It shattered and bitter quickfire pooled in my mouth, hungering for oxygen.

I exhaled, coating the conspirators in green flame. As they fell to the deck, my loyal crewers drew their blades. No trial and no ceremony—merely a purging of mutineers. All save Fiddich, who I buckled into the gibbet myself.

Corpses preserved in vacuum. Think what I could do with them! Ponda, we must befriend pirates!
—Dr. Evazan

FIFTH SIDEREAL CYCLE THE THIRTY-SEVENTH

Raise our mugs to fortune, and drain our mugs to victory! The first of Kanata's treasures lies in the belly of the *Bloody Bones*—a glittering pool of meleenium, hyperbarides, and prismatic crystals.

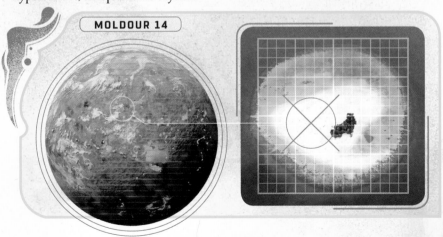

MOLDOUR 14

We set the droids to digging as soon as Poppy found the right sinkhole on the correct island on Moldour 14. The rays of sunup revealed the glint of metal at the bottom of the sandy pit.

Fur-Bite unsealed the vault and took a saberdart to the neck. But the other traps failed to fire.

I steered the *Bloody Bones* away from Moldour, corusca gems jangling in my pockets and laughing at Fiddich's remains hanging from a forward cannon. When the *Bones* lurched into hyperspace, Fiddich's bones scattered across the fiend-haunted void. **Noooo!**
—Dr. Evazan

FIFTH SIDEREAL CYCLE THE FORTY-FIRST

Today, we chart our course for the second Kanata treasure. Yet a shadow on the aft sensor troubles me. I fear it is the Dharus Buccaneers skulking in our wake. I will not suffer them to steal my prize.

FIFTH SIDEREAL CYCLE THE FORTY-THIRD

Our pursuer has drawn near enough to show his colors, but it is no Dharus pirate. Hawson says this one is a privateer drawing coin from the governor of the Maldrood Oversector. A pirate in the pay of another is a bilious vermin.

FIFTH SIDEREAL CYCLE THE FORTY-FOURTH

We shall not run from the likes of a privateer for even a day. We take aim and prime the cannons for firing.

This one wants a fight? Then a fight we shall have. The Pirate Queen Gunda Mabin does not flee.

FOR CENTURIES, THE MOONS OF MOLDOUR HAVE BEEN THE PLACE TO STASH YOUR STUFF. CAN'T HARDLY STICK A SHOVEL IN THE DIRT WITHOUT CLANGING AGAINST SOMETHING METALLIC. —APHRA

33

KRASTIC TARTA, THE PROLIFERATING HORROR

THOSE WORDS ARE BIGGER THAN ANY WORDS IN THIS BOOK SO FAR. THEY ARE BIGGER THAN ANY WORDS THERE WILL EVER BE!

A SLAVE READ THIS BOOK TO ME. ANOTHER SLAVE IS WRITING DOWN THE WORDS I SPEAK. I CAN DO ALL THOSE THINGS MYSELF, BUT WHY SHOULD I? I HAVE SLAVES AND MONEY.

WHAT I WANT IS MORE POWER. I AM KEEPING THIS BOOK.

NO ONE ELSE WILL FIND ITS TREASURES, GET SMARTER AND RICHER THAN KRASTIC TARTA—ESPECIALLY THE ZYGERRIANS. IT STAYS HERE ON THE ARKANIAN DAWN.

I AM THE SLAVEMASTER OF THE ARKANIAN DAWN AND I AM NOT LEAVING THIS PLANET YET. I HAVE DECIDED THERE IS WEALTH HERE.

THE WRECK OF A PIRATE SHIP AND A PRIVATEER RAIDER IS WHY I STOPPED AT THIS NO-NAME ROTBALL IN THE FIRST PLACE. THAT PRIVATEER'S EMERGENCY BEACON, CRYING FOR HELP IN EVERY DIRECTION! NOT CARING WHO HEARS AND NOT KNOWING THE KIND OF PEOPLE WHO WOULD ANSWER DISTRESS CALLS OUT HERE.

I GOT THERE BEFORE THE ZYGERRIANS, BUT FOUND NO ONE ALIVE IN EITHER SHIP. NO NEW SLAVES. JUST THIS BOOK AND WHATEVER PARTS THE SLAVES COULD STRIP FOR PROFIT.

BUT THE WHIPMASTERS SAW SOMETHING STRANGE. WORKING ALONGSIDE THE SLAVES WERE THE PURPLE ONES. NEW SPECIES: SIX ARMS, THICK FUR, LONG LEGS, BIG EYES.

NATIVES OF THIS PLACE, WORKING WITH OUR SLAVES, DOING THE SAME JOB. TRYING TO HELP THEM! IT IS TOO EASY TO CAPTURE THE ONES WHO ARE LIKE THAT. THAT IS WHY WE WILL STAY HERE. SEVEN VILLAGES ON THIS PIECE OF LAND AND KRASTIC TARTA CAN RAID THEM ALL IN JUST A FEW DAYS. THE NATIVES DON'T HAVE BLASTERS. THE HUNTING WILL BE GOOD.

THE HUNTING WAS GOOD. THE HOLDS OF ARKANIAN DAWN ARE FULL. THE NATIVES ARE STRONG, BUT THEY FLINCH WHEN I RAISE MY FIST. THEY DON'T SPEAK BASIC BUT WILL BE GOOD FOR LABOR, FIGHTING, AND SIMPLE JOBS.

THE ARKANIAN DAWN WILL REACH THE SLAVE MARKETS OF CHALCEDON SOON. THE WEAKEST ONES WILL BE DEAD BY THEN, LEAVING ONLY THE STRONG. KRASTIC TARTA WILL GET A GOOD PRICE FOR THE STRONG.

IT IS GOOD I FOUND THAT PLANET. THIS LOG BRINGS ME GOOD FORTUNE.
WITH THE MONEY FROM THE SLAVES, I WILL GET ANOTHER SHIP. AND ANOTHER. I WILL RULE THE
THALASSIAN GUILD INSTEAD OF THAT DOGSPITTLE IN CHARGE NOW. I WILL CRUSH THE ZYGERRIANS TOO.
THEY WILL ALL KNOW THE NAME KRASTIC TARTA, THE PROLIFERATING HORROR.

MY STORY IS JUST BEGINNING.

VARCINIUS AGGLOMERATION

The Galaxy's Most Complete Collection of Art, Artifacts, Folklore, and Biologicals

BENEFACTOR: Varcinius, 72nd of His Line
ARCHIVAL TAG, VARCINIUS REPOSITORY ON CLERION
ITEM NO. 7883001-112
DESCRIPTION: Spacers' recordkeeping journal (single volume, bicast polymer and paper)
CATEGORY: Esoterica
PURCHASE: Cyklo market, Chalcedon, Tashtor sector. Varcinius Acquisition Fund.

ACQUISITION HISTORY: Item encountered in Chalcedon slave market by bid buyer no. 14 (Varcinius Auction and Artifact Collective no. 8) while evaluating newly discovered alien specimens. Item acquired from Black Sun slavemongers at no charge in exchange for the bulk purchase of 22.5 kg of Whiphid ivory (52,500-credit expenditure).

ITEM HISTORY: Previous owner claims to have taken item from the body of one Krastic Tarta, a Thalassian slaver also known as "the Proliferating Horror." Tarta's cargo seems to have staged a slave revolt after touchdown on Chalcedon, seizing Tarta's ship *Arkanian Dawn*. Item's prior chain of ownership can be inferred from the log entries, with presumed originator being Maz Kanata (see Varcinius database *Personages of Note*, tier Alpha-X).

STORAGE RECOMMENDATION: Vacuum slab 0.35m x 0.40m, Beskar vault cylinder 551, slot 54.

RECORDED BY: Chuppa Chok, scrivener.

Recording this info for the boss, who says we should document our heists. Recording things is the only way to prevent data duplication and improve in our trade. Seems like a good way to get caught, but with the rest of the stuff in this book who would care about a heist.

No idea why this logbook was being held in the Varcinius Repository on Clerion, but because we were paid to steal the whole hexvault we ended up scooping this thing too.

> Loonoo—less commentary, more content. Thinner is contacting the client to arrange payment. Please use this time to analyze the Varcinius job and determine how to optimize future thefts. —Gallandro

Gallandro? Guess he had his fingers in all kinds of jobs before signing on as the CorpSec's hired gun. —Han

THE CREW:

» Gallandro, as boss (30% share)

» Loralynn Wheeler, as stick jockey (10% share)

» Banden Starshaper, as seal-cracker (8% share); note: formerly of Marso's Demons

» Nersiton, as slicer (12% share)

» Honest Loonoo, as fixer (20% share)

» Thinner Prokov, as interference (10% share)

» Kilitz and Kling, the Twins, as burglars (5% share each); note: veteran tunnelers from the Malkite land grab

THE SITE:

Varcinius "vault saucer" Repository in geostationary orbit between mesospheric cloud layers on Clerion (uninhabited gas giant in the Lower Tion).

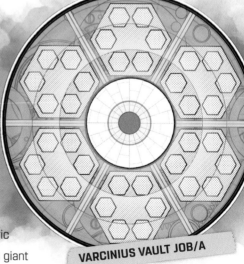

VARCINIUS VAULT JOB/A

THE PRIZE:

The Codeleach: the jewel-encrusted skeleton of a Metellos wyrdwyrm. 50 cm tall and held together with kiirium soldering. Payment offered by client: 1,575,000 credits.

THE PRE-JOB:

Chatter on the nets seeded by Thinner, hinting that small-batch scented gasses were fetching huge prices from criminal collectors. After the boss paid some Devaronian raiders for a smash-and-grab, they hit a gas shipment on its way to Varcinius cold storage. Now alerted to the possibility of a heist, the Varcinius archivists on Clerion rotated Hexvault Ring C to move the artisanal gasses into a higher-security zone near the hub.

[This action also rotated our true target into the lower-security periphery. We can duplicate this tactic against similar vaults. —Gallandro]

THE JOB:

Loralynn bounced the freighter off the planet's atmosphere, releasing a canister of buzz droids before angling back into space. The droids swarmed the saucer and drilled randomly at its hull. A few were captured and harmlessly exploded when they were brought inside, as planned. The speck-trackers released in the explosions began passively recording the ambient temperature, giving Nersiton the readings he needed to program the Twins' bodysuits so they wouldn't trip the station's thermal alarms.

The Twins, fired from the freighter's airlock, dropped through the cloud layers and deployed stellarsails as they neared the vault saucer.

[They used no tech of any kind. The station was wired to detect that. —Gallandro]

The Twins took five minutes to saw through the outflow grate and three minutes to crawl to Hexvault C. By following the diagrams Banden had drawn on their forearms, the Twins decoupled the hexvault and stood clear as the entire section fell from the station into the clouds below. Ten kilometers down, Loralynn successfully snagged the hexvault with the freighter's tractor beam.

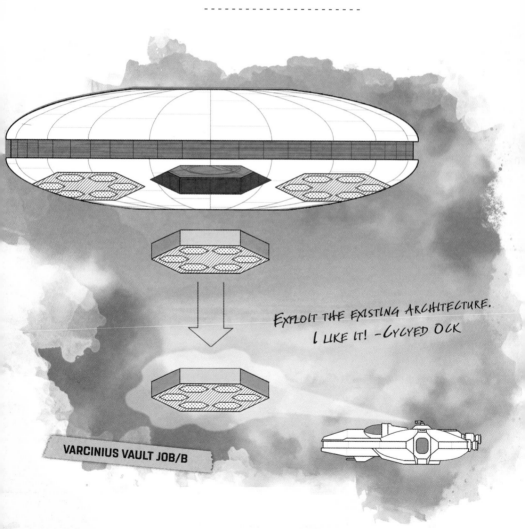

EXPLOIT THE EXISTING ARCHITECTURE.
I LIKE IT! —CYCYED OCK

VARCINIUS VAULT JOB/B

> After free-falling to the same spot, the Twins may have experienced some distress upon discovering the freighter was no longer in position to pick them up. During their long drop to the planet core, I hope they remembered how I told them that I don't like working with Malkite poisoners. —Gallandro

Boss says we've got another job lined up already. This time it's protection and enforcement, meaning I've got to line up a new crew.

THE SITE: *Nothing good ever happens on Savareen. —Han*

Savareen, Outer Rim. Dry Gulch settlement in the southern hemisphere. There's an independent coaxium refinery getting muscled by the Bellwing Gang (no syndicate affiliation, thankfully).

THE CREW:

Need at least twelve gunslingers to cut down the Bellwing Gang and chase any survivors offplanet. Starship ownership a plus.

> No more than six gunslingers, surely. I can assure you that no raw-boned Rimmer can outdraw me. —Gallandro

THE PAYMENT:

Only 10,000, but the locals say they'll let us tap the raw coaxium.

> I had not viewed the earlier pages of this logbook until just now. One of the treasure caches is said to lie beneath the Savareen wastes. We should investigate it at the very least. —Gallandro

Yeah, that never happened and for that I'm sorry, Gallandro. You were an okay boss most of the time.

"Honest Loonoo," that's what I go by. What did he think would happen once I learned this book might have some real value?

I joke about that descriptor, "Honest." But you'd be surprised: half the marks take it at face value. The other half know you're playing them, but they can't help but give you credit anyway for being upfront about it.

After hightailing it out of Savareen with the log, I worked my way back to Nar Shaddaa. This is home, the Smugglers' Moon, even though it stinks of waste and the sweat of a thousand species. The stench in the Corellian Sector is even worse than I remember, which means they haven't cleared those corpses from Level 42.

My room here isn't much, just a ventilation gap in the sublevels underneath a restaurant aquarium. My rib-cats missed me, I think, but given all the rat bones I had to brush off my cot I think they did okay. No more long cons like that Gallandro job! I'm sticking close to home from now on.

This log doesn't look like much, but I wager I could sell it for a fair bit of scrip, provided it's the real deal.

Spent most of today out at the spaceport. I'm old enough to remember the Jedi and the stories they told about the Sith. If the Force balances the dark and the light like they say, then the rest of us must get sorted into the smart and the stupid. In my experience, the second category is a lot bigger than the first.

Con games don't hurt anybody, not really. I get money, and they get taught not to fall for con games. Take my favorite scam. I'm selling acceleration couches to wide-eyed space jockeys and I've got the brochure to prove it, and sooner or later some captain agrees to stand at the foot of the boarding ramp holding one end of a string, while I hold the other to measure the interior of his freighter. As soon as I pass out of his line of sight I pocket whatever I can grab.

Today that was a book of Aargau credit certificates and a flask of Savareen brandy. And so, my rib-cats, let us drink a toast to the gullible!

Spaceport security has started paying more attention all of a sudden. Somebody in the cartels must have missed a payment.

No word yet from my authenticator on whether the images I sent from this log look legit. In the meantime, my kitties are crying. I know a store that sells vitablox for 35 creds a bag. How can I say no to so many flashing eyes?

Just don't try it on an undercover ISB agent. Harsh lesson at an early age. —Lando

Ashes

Molly

Mixie

Grish

Smokey

This district always had rib-cats, but then the shops started laying down paw spikes to shoo them off. My place doesn't have any paw spikes and it seems like more cats show up every day.

When I'm trying to sleep, I watch dark shapes swim in the blue glow above. Needlebaskers bunching up in dense schools and spiky krastiks marching the perimeter. The Mon Cal octopod is pretty shy, but it lashes its tentacles when it's hunting time.

The hum of the seawater circulators is nice too. Helps block out the whine of the swoop engines every time the Bloodfin Hellions race back to their garage in the last hour before dawn.

Is this why there are so many rib-cats running wild in the Corellian district? I've lost count of how many I've allowed aboard my ship.
—Sana Starros

///////

Need money. Thought about pickpocketing using the "Sorry, sir, let me clean up that sauce stain" bit, but chances are good I might get slugged. I'm also not going to do that "sell something and deliver an inferior version" scam, not after the last time when that Lasat discovered too soon that his nugget of Haysian smelt was actually a rock in metallic wrapping.

A couple days ago, I seeded the restaurant scam again, sending a medical bill to a hundred random food joints and claiming their stuff made me sick. This time only two of them actually paid up. This district might be getting wise to me.

Anyway, I made enough to buy the vitablox with enough left over for a bowl of purlah soup. Back in the day, it used to have a boiled momong head in it, but at some point, they replaced it with a chunk of bread that's molded to look like a head. Probably better this way. I left the broth out for the rib-cats.

///////

My neck hurts worse than yesterday, so I finally caved in and bought one of those elixirs from the bazaar at Salvage Station. But I didn't feel any different. It's just rainwater mixed with metal shavings, I bet.

LIVING FORCE ELIXIR

EMULSIFYING SOLUTION 60%, KYBER EX-
TRACT 5%, ROOTLEAF OIL 18%, CLARIT VITAE
13%, OSSAN ALCOHOL 4%, MINT DISTILLA-
TION FOR FLAVOR.

I thought he was one of the real ones, one of the lost Padawans grown older, maybe. It's always a bitter brew when a scammer gets scammed.

SHOULD HAVE CHECKED OUT SAL STA #42, FRIEND. SOME ARTIFACTS ARE LEGITIMATE, BUT YOU'VE GOT TO KNOW WHAT YOU'RE LOOKING FOR. —Aphra

I need a big score to keep my rib-cats in comfort. The spice den scam, probably.

/////

Well the spice den scam is off the table, thanks to those two ingrates.

Lentsch owns a spice den in Megablock 65, and Afflas is a friendly Zeltron who can turn any spacer's head. So, when she hooks an offworlder she invites him to a nice-looking spice den and convinces him to order an off-menu sampler. Lentsch brings out the cheap stuff before hitting him with a bill that's ten times what he was expecting—along with a warning to pay up or lose a limb.

It's a nice little scam; in fact it's so nice that those two decided they could run it without me. Even though it was my idea.

My authenticator still hasn't gotten back to me, which might mean this log is valuable and they've decided to snatch it for themselves. On my way home tonight, I caught some faces staring at me a little too long. You can't trust anyone.

/////

I'm positive somebody is closing in on me. I may have to abandon this residence.

I've rigged the base of the aquarium with balls of detonate, linked to a handheld trigger. When I push it, the tank will shatter and flood my place with 200 cubic meters of salt water.

My cats will be okay; they mostly come around for meals anyway. And this time they'll have all the fish they can eat!

/////

I know Bammy Decree can get me off Nar Shaddaa without going through customs, as long as I pay upfront. I don't have enough.

This might be the end of my line with this logbook if I can find a buyer who'll pay cash on the spot.

SKRRLL

(KEEP PRACTICING MY TAG. JAGGED EDGES = DANGER!)

KNEW HANGING OUTSIDE BAMMY'S SPACEBARN WOULD PAY OFF!

KNOCKED AROUND SOME OLD GUY TODAY AND GRABBED HIS STUFF. HE WASN'T CARRYING MUCH, BUT GOT A LITTLE HARD CURRENCY AND A COUPLE FREE-TRADE INGOTS, THIS LOGBOOK, AND A CUSTOMER CARD FOR THAT ANIMAL EMPORIUM ON LEVEL 220.

ALMOST TOSSED THAT LAST THING, BUT THEN I SAW THIS TINY PREDATOR RUBBING UP AGAINST MY BOOT. A RIB-CAT, I THINK? REMINDS ME OF MY OLD HUSHSTALKER BRUTUX.

THIS ONE SEEMED TO PACK-BOND WITH ME. I'VE GOTTA BUY BLASTER AMMO, BUT RIGHT AFTER THAT I'M BUYING SOME RIB-CAT FOOD. I'VE NAMED HER WARM FACE.

EPHANT MON

AND Masse Goskey

M.G.A.E.E.M. intake, Ephant Mon recording

- Herloss HBt-4 hunting blaster, 880 credits
- TAU-6-23 "Blastermill" rotary cannon, 990 credits
- BlasTech Imperial heavy repeater, 2,700 credits
- TL-50 heavy repeater, 3,200 credits
- Czerka X-55 Riot Infiltrator, 1,995 credits

MASSE GOSKEY'S

ARMS EMPORIUM AND EXPLOSIVES MART

It's always a good time to stay protected. Save up to **50 PERCENT** on some of our most popular items, including lightweight carry blasters, assorted scatterguns, body armor, thermic lances, and detonate tape. Contact Masse Goskey's friendly associate Ephant Mon for availability.

LIMITED TIME OFFER!

All personal combat items are 25 percent off with the purchase of three or more. Simply mention code "MASSE" when buying.

- Tantel pulverizers
- Collapsible force pikes
- Crushgaunts
- Electro-shock prods
- Folding vibroshivs

I've got to move this merch because everything we picked up on Nar Shaddaa is illegal in sixty-six sectors. That means we've gotta sell this stuff to the syndicates: Crymorah, Black Sun, you know.

I've got to make a huge profit off this score. It's bad enough I got scratched by some animal after you rumbled that street hood on Nar Shaddaa, but then I get my skin ripped by an octopod's tentacle in some alleyway! It's like the Emperor's menagerie in that place!

I am recording vital statistics concerning the cargo we picked up on Nar Shaddaa. Your habit of commenting on everything I write down is a distraction and needlessly takes up space. Many pages in this log have already been filled up, and you have no budget that covers miscellaneous supplies.

- Merr-Sonn Munitions SX-21 scatterblaster, 2,250 credits
- Czerka VT-33d, 1,400 credits

  I knew Plug-Eye Maygo ripped me off! —Sana Starros
- BlasTech E-27 blaster rifle, 1,800 credits
- Lasat CJ-9 electrified bo-rifle, 1,100 credits
- BlasTech E-9D blaster carbine, 950 credits
- SoroSuub QuickSnap 36T blaster carbine, 900 credits
- Blackscale "Hall Sweeper" carbine, 1,100 credits
- BlasTech F-78 with doubler, 1,200 credits
- BlasTech EE-4 carbine rifle, 850 credits
- Trandoshan ACP array gun, 1,200 credits

During our arms exchange on Bonadan, I purchased a new writing stylus and a billy-bag of finely shredded savory sweetmeats. I could have bought a logbook, but I've already started in on this one.

- Z-8 heavy rotary laser cannon, 3,340 credits
- Troida LT998 Armor Incinerator, 6,100 credits
- Merr-Sonn M-40 Thunderbolt light repeating blaster, 3,100 credits
- Merr-Sonn Mark II medium repeating blaster cannon, 4,450 credits
- BlasTech F-Web repeating blaster, 8,500 credits
- Morellian MWC-35 Staccato Lightning repeating cannon, 3,350 credits

Hey nosey, why are you never around when I need to talk to you? I lined us up a buyer. A rep for the Pyke Syndicate wants to make an exchange out at the Wheel. Get your stuff together.

Splendid. I've organized our inventory from greatest potential profit to least, based on Undervine demand and historical analysis of the invisible market. Let's make some money.

Are you insane, you freak? You put the HK8 Sawtooth at the bottom? Those things are the hottest thing going for syndicate street fronters. If you knew this business like I do, I wouldn't have to tell you these things.

The HK8 has a low ammo capacity, overheats during rapid fire, and is widely considered ugly. This bubble will pop, and a buyer for the syndicates is too sharp to chase fashions. I hope you will take my recommendation to heart for the sake of the business.

Ugly? Yes. Cosigned. —Lando

Listen up, loser. We're selling the Sawtooth. In fact, bring as many as you can, and don't question me again.

Looking back, the HK8 pistol proved valuable after all. It leaves a good-sized wound in a humanoid torso. Fortunately for Masse Goskey, a blaster shot to that area isn't fatal for humans, is it?

MASSE GOSKEY'S
ARMS EMPORIUM
AND EXPLOSIVES MART

FORTY (40) BLASTER CARBINES:	56,999
TWELVE (12) RIOT GUNS:	17,999
TWO (2) TROIDA ARMOR INCINERATORS:	14,999
EXTENDED WARRANTY:	999
ONE (1) CASE HK8 SAWTOOTHS:	FREE TRIAL
POWER GAUNTLET GRAB-BAG (AS IS, NO REFUNDS):	11,000
TOTAL:	101,996

Pleasure doing business with you!

No, wait, I'm thinking of Ugors. Alas, Masse. Enjoy the Netherworld.

Now I just need to rework the name. Chevin Armorers? I'll come up with something.

- Merr-Sonn R-88 Suppressor riot rifle, 2,000 credits
- BlasTech 500 ESPO riot gun, 1,000 credits
- Gordarl Weaponsmiths LR1K sonic cannon, 9,000 credits
- Loronar ABX-110 Aural-Biological-Chemical scrambler, 3,000 credits
- Merr-Sonn GRS-1 snare rifle, 1,100 credits
- Arakyd X8 xenotoxic fléchette, ask for current market price

So what is this? Evidence of the gunrunner's extortion? Quite careless that his lieutenant left it inside that weapons crate, but that is why Cikatro Vizago will never hire a Swokes Swokes.

Looks like I paid at least 25 percent over wholesale. Nothing can be done for it now, but from now on I'll take every advantage I can get including this pawed-over journal. It is the only way I can elevate the Broken Horn syndicate into a regional power player.

CYNABAR'S INFONET
Always Bet on the Big CYN

WHO'S WHO IN THE LOTHAL SECTOR

CIKATRO VIZAGO

EXPERTISE:
Smuggling, extortion

AFFILIATION:
Broken Horn Gang *Syndicate! I told them syndicate!*

USER COMMENTS:
LomPaulsen: Tried to show off the weapons I was selling but his IG droids shot at me! Forget Vizago, there are loads of buyers on Garel.

AZMORIGAN

EXPERTISE:
Swindling, blackmail

AFFILIATION:
Independent

USER COMMENTS:
BonadanBouncer: Transported puffer pigs for this guy, he wouldn't pay for the cleanup. Avoid.
OakieP: He's a creep.

Broken Horn is much more than a gang, but by my own admission it's hardly a galactic syndicate. I need more than a piece of the smuggling out of Garel to ensure my legacy.

I keep putting the squeeze on the sector locals, but ever since the Empire took control, my slice of the action keeps getting thinner. Turns out these horns aren't exactly an asset when doing business under the New Order.

I've read the front pages of this journal and come up with a plan. Time to go treasure hunting: the target is Seylott. I need partners to help with infiltration and excavation.

Seylott's coordinates, as an exponent applied to Nar Shaddaa's coordinates, are an irrational product. I have entered this nonterminating string into my calculations.
—Master Codebreaker

Azmorigan has eyes everywhere, and I'm reasonably certain he won't stick a knife in my back, so he's in.

I'll still need someone to recover the treasure. Needs to be a surveyor and digger, not to mention a fast talker for when the heavies come sniffing around. That's the kind of face work I can't be bothered with. Luckily humans are plentiful, and Azmorigan knows an acceptable one that goes by the name of Calrissian.

We're making our move tomorrow. Azmorigan warned me to watch out for Black Sun operations in this sector. I told him I had it under control, but once he was out of earshot I ordered Calrissian to watch out for Black Sun operations in this sector.

Eternal rot! Black Sun has got this planet on lockdown. But we are merely three wanderers. Surely, we can venture into the restricted andris-mining zone to undertake a terrain survey. Why would Black Sun harass nomads? It's fine.

"Humans are plentiful"? Vizago, I'll have you know that Lando Calrissian is one of a kind. When Black Sun moved in waving their vibroaxes and shatterpicks, I was the only one sharp enough to stash this logbook and talk my way out of trouble.

"Those two are the brains," I cried out. "I'm just some guy they hired!" The best lie is usually the truth.

Shame that I've almost burned through my upfront fee, but first-class treatment in the Spiran mineral spas is the only thing that can soothe my nerves after such a trying ordeal. They say it takes a full day for a human to recover from a Sriluurian skin scrubbing, so I've had lots of time to peruse this lucky little logbook.

Maz Kanata, I knew you'd make me rich one day!

Just one lousy page? Knew I shouldnt have swung at that goon, but the urge to dazzle that Trianii debutante was too strong. —Lando

RAZZI SYNDICATE

[RAZZI] Submister Twirm: Verify the authenticity of this document. Tell me where it came from. Remember that I feed you, clothe you, and shield you from our enemies. Do you think Jabba would be so generous?

[TWIRM] My mistress: as requested. Previous owner, one Lando Calrissian. Item obtained following opportunistic beatdown by Prowling Thug 36 (Esoomian brawler Bumblethunk). Item lifted from Calrissian's person by Pickpocket 8 (Rybet thief "Sticky Fingers"). Cover bears the chevron colors of Maz Kanata's buccaneer sails, suggesting it is an authentic Kanata artifact.

CYNABAR'S INFONET

Always Bet on the Big CYN

When I get the power, the first thing I'm going to do is execute everyone at Cynabar's. Reporters? Evisceration. Editors? Disintegration - Razzi

OBA DIAH, OUTER RIM The Pyke Syndicate continues to flatten smaller criminal operations in its bid to become the galaxy's sole spice dealer.

Insiders have fingered Latts Razzi as the next player to feel the pinch, and Cynabar's analysts are doubtful that Razzi's organization can survive the challenge.

[RAZZI] I don't care about that. Tell me what I can do with it! Do you have a hole in your head?

[TWIRM] I am an Adarian, my mistress. My cranial aperture helps to focus and amplify sound waves.

[RAZZI] I am the boss of a crime cartel, which I thought would be enough to insulate me from noodling dullskulls, but no. Twirm—will this logbook help me or not? I can't put it any plainer.

[TWIRM] Mistress, I bring good tidings. Authentication results are on their way. In anticipation of a favorable outcome, I have prepared a team to retrieve the extant treasure caches indicated in this volume.

If I may beg the mistress's indulgence, it appears you are preoccupied with how the Latts Razzi crime family ranks versus other underworld players, particularly the Pykes. Might I make a suggestion? Act as if you hold more power than you actually do, and the underworld will respond accordingly. This trade is dominated by the insecure and the paranoid. Among such opponents, appearances are often more effective than reality.

[RAZZI] You're fired. And by fired, I mean fed to the undercrab. Appearances don't matter. What matters is ability.

By the time you read this, the Gamorreans will have arrived to escort you to the pit.

Until I hire a new submister, I'll have to keep this journal sidelined. Other matters demand my attention, and it's so hard to find good help in this business.

Razzi came to a bad end, didn't she, Chewie? Or maybe that's just wishful thinking. —Han

CATALOGUE NUMBER
9388GR/77

NOTES | *Qi'ra: exploit this item or dispose of it.*

*I asked Gremm to fast-track analysis of this logbook. Until then, I will con-
tinue to review incoming cargo from the Razzi warehouse raid with regard to
Crimson Dawn's business interests, until an underscribe can lift the data
impressions from these pages.* — **Qi'ra**

CRATE NUMBER
CRATE 40 3X

||||||||||||||||||

Glazed pottery vases with patterned imprints in the style of the Kitel Phard dynasty. Accompanying tablet bears the mark of the White Worms, Coronet, Corellia.

A single Kitel Phard vase could fetch 250,000 credits at auction, but all of these are fakes. Lady Proxima must be doing business with Latts Razzi's operation, which violates the terms of the White Worms' loyalty. Recommend <u>swift and merciless</u> retaliation to serve as a lesson to others.

Buttoned-up and ruthless.
That's you all over. —Han

||||||||||||||||||||||||||||||||||||||||||||||||

CRATE NUMBER
CRATE 20 3X

||||||||||||||||||

Small arms and mid-grade explosives. Nothing particularly notable about this cargo, but the HK8 Sawtooth has not yet entered mass production. Its presence here indicates that Razzi enjoys robust supply lines with gunrunners, which Crimson Dawn could presumably control.

||||||||||||||||||||||||||||||||||||||||||||||||

CRATE NUMBER
CRATE 43 9X

50 kg of low-grade andris spice, hidden inside spherical objects of Weequay religious veneration. Purity is poor. Razzi's organization must be sourcing from the Spice Triangle. Suggest squeezing Zorba the Hutt to see what he knows.

CRATE NUMBER
CRATE 32 7X

Disassembled HK-model gladiator droids bearing Grakkus medallions.

NOTE:
It has been reassembled to verify parts.

CRATE NUMBER
CRATE 51 7X

Exotic animal parts. Rancor fangs, aiwha sacs, shaved mynock silicate, sando tooth cuttings (2 m wide); dried octopod ink (15 mg vials); <u>two complete tu'kata specimens</u> (mummified, one pictured here), various Corellian hound components (spinal ridges, claws, fur tufts, hide patches).

Got a Shadow University buyer on Archaeo-Prime who'd pay big creds for these, if only I could cut myself into the supply line. —Aphra

Val found this log in the crate we nabbed from the freight platform in Zarra on Cato Neimoidia. Crate checked out. Crimson Dawn goods with Dryden Vos's seal. Railcar robbery is a go.

Bad news. Purseworld Security cares enough to profile us.

CLAIMED IDENTITY: VAL
SPECIES: HUMAN

CLAIMED IDENTITY: DURANT, RIO
SPECIES: ARDENNIAN

CLAIMED IDENTITY: TUSKA
SPECIES: MON CALAMARI

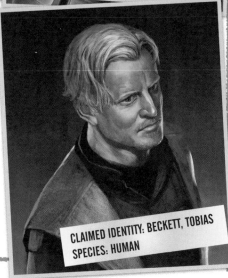

CLAIMED IDENTITY: BECKETT, TOBIAS
SPECIES: HUMAN

Okay, that did not work. **AT ALL**.

Let me start with Tuska, because he's the first of the many, many things that misfired on this operation. If we're going to hit a Railcrawler conveyex, we need a spotter who keeps his eyes open.

All Tuska had to do—and just somebody kill me already—was scale the 7 o'clock face of the Bride's Talon and keep watch for escorts. If it's hauling Crimson Dawn cargo, Cato Neimoidia security was going to be extra worried about bandits on the way to Tarko-se. So if you don't see any escorts through your macrobinocs, <u>maybe get on the comm and call in an abort</u>.

No escorts? That doesn't add up. I know Tuska can't do sums but this was kinda important. So here's me with no

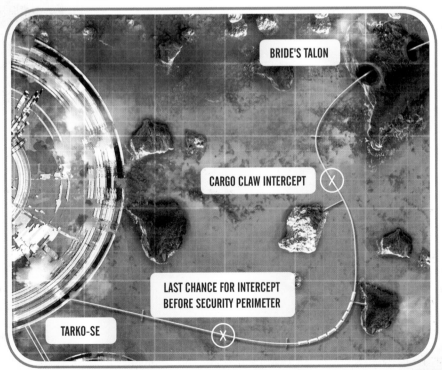

BRIDE'S TALON

CARGO CLAW INTERCEPT

LAST CHANCE FOR INTERCEPT
BEFORE SECURITY PERIMETER

TARKO-SE

warning, dropping from the freighter on a fibercord. I grab onto the conveyex and shuffle to the railcar coupling. This train is going 200 km/hr, so how the hell could I hear the whine of a swoop engine? Maybe because there were **MORE THAN A DOZEN OF THEM.**

Wish I'd known you were learning on the job, Beckett. Maybe Chewie and I would have kept a wide berth. —Han

This was Enfys Nest and her cloud riders, not some local gang. Rio angled the freighter and Val took potshots with the cannon. Took out—two of them? Maybe? Not even close to enough.

I'm still pressed up against the skin of the railcar, hanging on to the seams with my fingertips. Did a lot of cursing . . . maybe some praying.

The plan—let's all remember the PLAN—was to latch onto the rearmost railcar with the cargo claw and hoist it before we reached the city. I figured Enfys Nest had her own plan that maybe involved shooting out the tracks and sending the whole conveyex into the abyss. Don't know what they planned to steal, but they must have figured that getting it wet wouldn't hurt.

I jumped. Broke the water in a needle stance and kicked my way back to the surface. Nobody told me the water on Cato Neimoidia was acidic and now I think I burned out my taste buds.

So what did we learn, people? I learned you can burn a whole pit of money by funding a risky operation that falls apart from stupid mistakes.

We were in debt before. Now we're in triple debt.

LOOKING FOR SOMETHING?!
TOO SAD! YOUR SHIP IS NOW THE PROPERTY OF

BANDIT BILLIE

To a spacer, there's no lower form of guttersnipe than a shipjacker. —Sana

I switched packs with that old guy in Zarra. Now he's carrying a bunch of rocks and a plaque with my calling card on top. Okay I stole his pack, not his ship, but I can't be making templates for every karking thing.

Wasn't anything in his pack worth stealing anyway, just a vanachord I pawned for 45 creds. This paper-flipper right here, though? I like it and I'm squeezing it close. Good for practicing ink prints.

I can't shake a single sniff when it comes to smuggling or the syndicates, but I've already snapped to the thought that every one of these shadowports has got a stuffed landing pad and a babystyle security force. I'm a shipjacker, so I've got to start jacking some ships. I'm talking big ones.

I know how to spring the ships, but I don't have the hands to fly 'em. So today I looked up Ratty-Ratty, and she told me she's in with both feet. I got the vibe she'd been waiting for me to comm her again, ever since that time we both got collared at the Imp impound yard.

So she says, hey hire this other friend of mine too, Taurill somebody, and I say sure Ratty-Ratty but to steal an assault carrier we're gonna need a whole crew. And that's when she told me about Taurill, that they were like a hundred thieves cuz hive mind. Instead of calling her the night's darkest liar I said instead, how in the naked expanse am I gonna pay for a hundred crewers?

Today Ratty-Ratty brought Taurill aboard for a job interview and said they'll work for food. At first, I figured she had gotten right rolled about the whole "hive mind" thing, but then I whispered to the closest critter, I told them that joke about what the Emperor wears under his robes. And sure as I'm cycling, the whole room of fuzzles busted out laughing at once—even the ones in the back.

Hive mind, hey? I say Bandit Billie has got her crew.

We start shipjacking on Ryloth. Ratty-Ratty brought me this whole sheet about Kala'uun port traffic and docking slips and all of that crunch. So I said to her, you didn't have to do all this work just to get me to like you! And she squeaked and ran to her cabin, so another regular day here on Billie's ship.

IMAGE CAPTURE OF KALA'UUN PORT AUTHORITY

Kala'uun on Ryloth is one of those ports that slaps a boot on your landing strut, to stop ship theft they say. That's good for me, cuz those boots make port security feel okay with snoozing or boozing instead of looking out for shipjackers. Makes the whole job as simple as picking a bloom.

Long-face letdown! Taurill don't know scratch about cracking a boot shackle. They only know what you tell them, so mostly they've been leaving their little green droppings all over the hold. But now school's in session.

Seems to me like only a quarter of the Taurill actually do anything and the rest just fake it. That's pretty much everybody though, right?

Happy face! Just like I shimmied, cracking these ion boots is a cutout copy so silky even the Taurill can get it.

I've cracked baby boots like this a hundred times. Cut through the hydraulics here. Hold down the safety here. Disarm the poppers by squeezing this lever here. Rattle the time-lock tumblers with a vibram shaker, that's here. Then brute-force the seam right here. Easy pleezy.

Score scorez! Bandit Billie and her thrilly-billy crew are hauling feet away from Ryloth on a route nobody's gonna check! For as long as it lasts, I'm the captain of a Corellian assault carrier.

I told one of the Taurill to leave my spray on the tarmac so they'd know who did it but I forgot about the hive mind, though. They laid down three dozen sprays right on top of the other. Hope they can read one of 'em at least.

Negotiations: locked and cozy. Tomorrow Bandit Billie makes delivery to the Rebellion. I'll affirm on the holy rolls that this resistance against the Empire is gonna be very good for business.

Okay the Rebels, they aren't rich it turns out. We came out ahead on the trade but mostly cuz Taurill are square with eating the backalley trash that Ratty-Ratty scraped up on Ylesia. But where we can really get rich isn't military ships. It's pleasure yachts! And looky looky, those Ubrikkian models are all over this sector.

Could hive mind = flighted polymirroring of the data I've assembled thus far? Maz Kanata, you are indeed a devious one!
—Master Codebreaker

His Excellency Jabba Desilijic Tiure of Nal Hutta, Eminence of Tatooine

—Desilijic Kajidic—

Today's humble servant of the mighty Jabba is:

Bib Fortuna, Majordomo

That shipjacker has learned never to repeat her errors, provided she lives. I expect not. Wounds inflicted by a Gamorrean vibroax do not knit swiftly.

That mob of animals accosted the *Star Jewel* during the layover on Nar Haaska. Superficial damage to the landing gear and hull plating only, but more than enough for Jabba to notice.

Have changed course for Keldooine and a decent repair bay. Along the way, I hope to discern why such an inept thief clung to this book with such ferocity.

Saw this book in the waiting area of Keldooine Starshipwrights and thought it might help me out, but what's a guy like me supposed to do with it? I ain't a smuggler and I sure as scratch ain't a treasure hunter. Maybe three decades ago, back when my knees didn't pop and the underworld still made sense.

I've been posting this listing on the Undervine for a month without a nibble. How come nobody'll hire a mercenary anymore?

SAPONZA, SOLDIER FOR HIRE

EXPERIENCE:

Mytaranor Campaign, Kwymar Suppressions, Retreat from Parcelus Minor

SPECIALIZATIONS:

Blaster rifles, blaster pistols, front-line infantry tactics, vibro-bayonets, short-range artillery, squad command

REFERENCES:

Available upon request

Crimson Dawn? Nothing! Son-Tuul Pride? Nothing! They've all got their own private armies, I figure.

I need some credits fast if I'm gonna lose that Mando assassin. I'm telling you, you skip out on Black Sun ONE TIME, and this is what happens!

I knew I recognized that gray binding. Maz Kanata, what were you thinking by sending this out into the wild?

I've never run with pirates, but I know the smuggling biz well enough to know the secrets in this book are too valuable for just anybody. Look who's owned it before me! Cheaters, grifters, and lowlifes, not to mention Lando.

If the Empire got this, you could say goodbye to those shadowports. That's why it's staying right here with me: smuggler extraordinaire Platt Okeefe.

I mean, I'll get to that level eventually. Right now, I got a freighter, a droid mechanic, and not much else. I'm a quick study, though.

It's not like I'm against sharing secrets of the smuggling trade. If I wrote my own guide, I'd only share it with people who knew their stuff. Completing 5 Sisar Runs = basic access. 3 Kessel Runs = advanced access.

There's a LOT out there that raw spacers don't know, and I hate to see anybody fail. There's too much pettiness in this business already.

Oakie is one of the good ones. —Sana

PROFITABLE SMUGGLING CARGOES:

For example, I'm not crazy about how Maz presented this. There's absolutely a payoff in megonite moss, but possession of the stuff is a class 1 felony. Instead, smugglers should try hauling these:

- Aurodium: Brentaal Trading Houses. Ask for Pinnace at any boot polisher.
- Greel wood: Pii system. Seek out the lumberdroid with the slipshod tread and use passcode O623N37.
- Oro-weave: Chandrila. Ask for Ox-Herder at the Trappist cantina on Guildhead's Way.

Other cargoes that turn a profit: meleenium, durelium, and hyperbarides. Corusca stones, Mandalorian beskar, quella gems, and prismatic crystals. There's spice of course, but stick with andris, carsunum, or sansanna and never mess around with ryll or the prime Kessel strains.

Review the exchange feeds that come in from the Corporate Sector and price your goods accordingly. There's no shame in honest profiteering! *Buy low, sell high*: that's the smuggler's mantra.

PICK YOUR HAULER:

Skip the Gymsnor, the TL-1200, or anything from Balmorran Heavyworks. Look to these models for reliable and speedy tramp freighters on the cheap.

- **GHTROC 720:** my sentimental fave
- **LANTILLIAN SHORT HAULER:** the spacer's "old reliable"
- **SURRONIAN L19 HEAVY FREIGHTER:** buy used, never new unless you know a good mechanic
- **YT-2400:** hot tip: there's decommissioned models tumbling through the Zero Drift; if you slip past the void-droids you can boost one for free!

SHADOWPORTS AND BOLTHOLES:

Maz's list is a good start. I'd add:

- Junkfort Station
- Port Bianco
- Byblos (of course)
- Dandrian Ring
- Gelgelar Free Port
- Resh 9376 (remember to bring your own atmospheric supply)
- Tanquilla Beach

Despite what you hear, avoid Omze's Incredible Traveling Starport, especially if you're a human. Black Spire Outpost on Batuu isn't exactly a shadowport, but you can find all sorts of interesting things for sale if you know who to ask.

SMUGGLING CLIENTS:

These employers will hire freelancers, but don't expect them to treat you friendly if you botch a run.

- **GLASFIR RING:** on the upswing, cozy with the Empire
- **KLATOOINIAN TRADE GUILD:** will pay half upfront if you negotiate
- **MANDROXAN CARTEL**
- **ORORO TRANSPORTATION:** fronted by Tenloss syndicate, friendly with the Rebellion
- **KHEEDAR RING**
- **DROID GOTRA:** you know what, never mind
- **LANTILLIAN SPACERS' BROTHERHOOD:** does business with anti-Imperial guerrillas like Gerrera's Partisans—could be lucrative for gunrunners who don't mind risking a treason charge

IMPERIAL SPACE MINISTRY
BUREAU OF SHIPS AND SERVICES

CAPTAIN'S ACCREDITED LICENSE   FORM# LIC5510.02

NAME
OKEEFE, PLATT

SPECIES
HUMAN

HOMEWORLD
BRENTAAL IV

CAPTAIN'S ACCREDITED LICENSE NUMBER
AGG-99301-BH05CT

STARSHIP CLASSIFICATION
LIGHT FREIGHTER

PILOT SIGNATURE

Platt OKeefe

LICENSED SHIPPING:

A savvy smuggler can slide into legit cargo hauling at the first hint of a customs crackdown. You've got to get your accreditations from the Bureau of Ships and Services and the Imperial Space Ministry, and keep them current. Always flash your documentation if you're boarded by Imperials.

CHALMUN'S CANTINA

ꟻꗃꓘꓘꓓꓥꓩ'ꗃ ꟻꓘꓘꓥꓕꓩꓘꓘ

RED DWARF

POLANIS RED & MANDALLIAN NARCOLETHE
WITH RECIRCULATED FIZZWATER

CASSANDRA SUNRISE

MERENZANE GOLD & ZABRAK FERMENT,
FLAVORED WITH LACHRYMEAD AND
GARNISHED WITH A VAPORATOR MUSHROOM

NOVA BLASTER

CORELLIAN BRANDY & IPELLRIA FIREWATER,
MIXED IN A CENTRIFUGE

FLAMEOUT

HULL-STRIPPER & VASCHEAN RYE SERVED IN
A JET-JUICE FLASK

WATCH OUT FOR:

Picket fleets, territorial police, pirate raiders, and military blockades.

I should add something about avoiding capture long enough to jump to hyperspace. I've been hearing about Imperial Interdictors—cruisers that use gravity generators to block hyperspace entry—which is something that could void all the existing rules.

THE SECRET MENU:

All the busiest spaceports have watering holes that cater to our trade. But almost nobody knows the passcodes that will give you prime access to black-market gear.

Take Chalmun's Cantina in Tatooine's Mos Eisley spaceport. They'll look at you funny if you ask for a drinks list but do it anyway, then order a Nova Blaster with Savareen brandy swapped for Corellian. You'll get escorted behind the bar and into their hidden gun closet.

So far, everything I've written looks pretty good! There's definitely enough material for me to get started on a comprehensive guide of my own. First, though, I'm going to offload this Jovanian gorefruit. This is another profitable cargo, because the Jovanians only plant groves on the galaxy's bloodiest battlefields. They believe the fruit blesses their limbs with murderous might.

I've been hired to deliver the gorefruit to a drop-point agent on Panna's Redwater moon. I'm feeling pretty good about it, since there's a chance parlor in the Offworlders' Block I've been itching to visit again.

Not after they changed it. Last I heard, you've gotta ask for a Gruvian spice-ice. —Han

Well well well, what have we here? A book that leaves my hands and returns all on its own. It's true what they say—Lando Calrissian can't lose.

If only Platt Okeefe could say the same! She knew what she was getting into when she agreed to play pazaak against a master of the cards, and Oakie always had a weakness for Norvanian grog. I played an honest game, no matter what she shouted as I hustled back to the *Falcon*.

Time to take stock. 5,500 credits from the Boarbeetle on Panna for delivering sweet seasow milk (not nearly enough, considering how fast the stuff spoils). Add to that the 603 credits from Oakie in the final pot, plus her Herglic chronometer and this logbook.

Not to worry, we made up. At the Far Orbit bathhouses, I believe. —Lando

I took a second look through this book with the benefit of a sober head. This could be big. If Maz Kanata laid down coordinates for these treasure vaults, they're definitely out there.

Mama Calrissian's boy could finally get the respect he deserves! Should probably skip the treasure on Seylott, though. I'm betting that Vizago fouled it up beyond salvaging.

I've got plenty of experience recovering relics, but I'm not a one-man show. I need a navigator. A hauler. A lock picker. (Maybe the Tonnika sisters? At least the one who doesn't hate me right now. Maybe?) That's a lot of fees to shell out upfront, and no friend of mine still takes my promises on credit. Time for me to do what I'm best at.

Gambling is high risk and high reward, so it automatically screens out the galaxy's worst idiots. You might think that most planetary governments have outlawed casino gambling, but a lot of the time there's a pleasure barge orbiting just outside governmental jurisdiction. And there's always a game of hazard toss in the backrooms of spaceport cantinas.

BETTER THAN A SKIFTER!
INVISIBLE TO WAVESCANS!

Entirely mechanical, this grabber lets you pluck cards from the deck and return them to your hand.

The latest innovation from SquibLabs will turn your luck around— guaranteed!

With this miracle, who needs Lady Fate?

MILLENNIUM F

Feast your eyes on the Millennium Falcon. Looks like a million credits on the outside, and the interior is getting there. The galaxy has plenty of Corellian Engineering YT-1300 freighters, but none of them are my baby.

I suppose you want me to install these new modifications?

No, why would I expect you to work, L3? Just keep doing what you're doing. Remind me: what is it that you do again?

Please indicate the specifications for what you have termed a "wet bar." I can set the ship's atmospheric humidity to 95 percent but I can't guarantee you'll find it comfortable.

That's it! At the next starport, I'm lifting off without you. Good luck finding another master who'll put up with you.

Good luck finding another droid who can duplicate my hyperspace calculations.

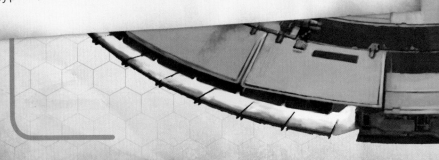

HTER

ALCON

3—this could be made into a clothes closet
too. When have I ever gotten sick?—*Lando*

So . . . which casinos haven't banned me yet? Relatta, Pavo Prime, the Oseon, Zirtran's . . .

Then again, there's always Canto Bight. It's got the tightest security anywhere, but hobnobbing with high society is where I'm at my best.

I've got to be at my best in a place like Canto Bight. Time for *The Calrissian Chronicle*'s six-part philosophy for disaster-proof high rolling.

Look the part. Anyone can pass through the ropes if they look like they belong. Each casino attracts a different class of customer, so copy that look and walk with confidence to the big-money tables. Wear a cape to say, "I've got family money." I've got a royal velvet infraweave number that lets me pass for a solar-yacht heir, so long as no one asks me anything about sailing.

You can beat the house, but you can't beat the house twice. As soon as you haul in a bank-breaking score at the tables, you're on a list. Don't rack up multiple big wins in the same night—let the casino owners save face—and think twice before returning under the same identity.

Set your own limits. Before you walk through the doors, decide how much you're prepared to lose. In my case that's usually an amount many times greater than what I actually possess, but then again I'm comfortable with those odds.

know at least one match that proves you a liar, old buddy. —Han

Master the rules of the game. Don't sit at the table until you've learned the stock rules, the house rules, the regional variant rules, and all of the unspoken etiquette concerning the placing and raising of bets. If you don't know enough to split a pairing in riftwalker sabacc and double your bet against a dupe or a face card, you shouldn't be sitting there in the first place.

Use the comps. At a casino you can enjoy free drinks, provided you tip well. And free food, provided you remember which dishes at the buffet are toxic to your species. Or a free room, provided you make the right kind of friend. These might be the only transactions where you can actually beat the casino.

They cheat you, you cheat them right back. Sometimes the house cheats. I've seen loaded dice, a weighted wheel, a false shuffle, and a programmed randomizer. At a crooked Quaymoon betting parlor in Hutt Space, it's practically your moral obligation to cheat. Train a partner to send nonverbal signals from across the table. And while I don't believe in lucky charms, nervously fiddling with one will draw the dealer's eye long enough for you to slip a 1,000-credit chip into the middle of your winning stack.

CANTO BIGHT

CANTONICA

FORTUNE'S BLESSINGS SHOWER UPON THE CASINO FLOOR, where daring risk-takers and elegant sophisticates win in spectacular fashion. Canto Bight offers the quintessential gambling experience, with traditional games and sector favorites alongside the newest sensations from the Core to the Rim.

TABLE GAMES

CARDS AND TILES: Horansi, Savareen Whist, Chambers, Pazaak, Liar's Cut, Desert Draw, Klikklak, Highland Challenge, Uvide, Zhell Reversal, Sabacc (Centran and Empress Teta Preferred variants)

WHEEL: Jubilee Wheel, Spinner-Pit, Greehu Wheel

STRATEGY: Shah-Tezh, Dejarik, Moebius, Triga

DICE: Chance Toss, Divot, Fantafly, Hintaro, Corellian Spike

Zhell Reversal could be the one! It's new in their sector and it has some rules that can be exploited without forcing a cheat. Count the cards in the dealer's stack. Triple your bet when the split is between seven and eleven. Cut your bet in half at a consecutive card, double if you can cover the spread, and fold if the dealer turns up a Redbird.
—Lando

In other words, invert the data markers after every versal flag. I grow ever closer to decoding this textual cipher.
—Master Codebreaker

88

SPORTS BETTING

Live Fathier Racing
Odupiendo Racing
Core Circuit Grav-Ball
All-Class Shockboxing
Roon Drainsweeper

Need an inside agent before making this kind of risk. A perfect trifecta in the fathier races could set me up for life. —Lando

MACHINE GAMES

Declination
Starcourse
Shronker
Thornen Pyramid
All the latest and hottest
Randomizer Machines offering the biggest payouts

You can change the odds on these machines with a cyborg cranial band, but most casinos figured that out a long time ago. No way I'm hiring a Suerton again. "Subconscious control over probability"? 12,000 in wasted tokens says otherwise, pal. —Lando

To Lando, my love, I will always cover your escapes.
—The Duchess Reina Sarapinia

Found this logbook in a chance parlor on Makem Te with that card on top of it. She probably thought he'd come back, but it looks like my buddy Lando jumped clear out of the sector. Clear skies, Lando.

Seems like Maz started this. I'll return it to her the next time I'm around Takodana way. She'll appreciate that. Pretty sure she's got a thing for me.

Bunch of stick jockeys and star-skaters in here, boasting when all they've really done is dig at the dirt and shoot at each other. A fueled-up engine and an open horizon, that's all anybody needs.

Yep, that's me, young BoShek. First place in the Malastare Classic, flying a double-barreled Zephyr-K welded out of junkyard scraps. They say humans can't compete at those speeds, but I think they're just afraid of the competition.

RACING DIGEST

Just got the word that my application was accepted for the Dragon Void Rally, one of the most prestigious races in the Rim Territories. No Corellian has won it in a century, but I'm breaking that streak this year.

It'll take a week to get there, at a low gear so I can keep my engine tuned. Gives me lots of time to go through my lockers. That *Racing Digest* clipping made me nostalgic for the old days. I guess that's why I've been recording so much.

Look at this—the swoop race through the crystal forests of Agrilat. I remember I had first place locked up, flying a modified Mobquet with an overtuned engine and illegal aftermarket boosters.

Dramatic Finish at Agrilat

I had it in the bag, drifting in the slipstream of the leading swooper and waiting to thumb the booster to overtake him on the wide turn. But he flashed his engine baffles and dumped coolant into the thrust exhaust. The fireball got bigger and bigger as I flew into it.

It was either get roasted or bite it, so I nosed my swoop down into the oil slick below. Nearly drowned. Spent two weeks in a medcenter so they could pump slurry out of my lungs and racking up debt that I couldn't possibly pay.

HUMAN RACER CLINGS TO LIFE

How could I? I was only good at one thing: racing. *I can outrace you any day, pal. —Han*

• ○ ○ ◯ ○ ○ •

Nearly arrived at the Dragon Void. Racing a starship isn't like racing a speeder bike—you've got all of three-dimensional space to maneuver in, which doesn't always make for compelling holocam footage. That's why race organizers always try to force competitors onto the same plane by bottlenecking the course between narrow obstacles. If the race is sponsored by a syndicate, expect space mines to fire live laser charges.

Lazy race organizers try to capture some good footage at the starting line, and then they pack the rest of the broadcast with inspirational stories.

This Troig hopes to open a diner with the winnings! Meet the Devlikk who's being cheered on by his three spouses and thirty-five offspring!

That might be racing to some, but not to me. I'm BoShek. If you want to know my story, just keep your eye on the finish line.

• ○ ○ ◯ ○ ○ •

SALTBITE'S RACING FORM:
WHAT TO LOOK FOR WHEN BETTING ON A SKI SPEEDER

That's from when I raced the ski speeder circuit for a single season in the Geister belt. Made enough to pay off my creditors.

Was just thinking that if I win, place, or show in the Dragon Void, I'll have enough to fund my next move. I've had an idea for a long time about threading the Corkscrew through the Thunderhead, cutting a bit chunk off the Kessel Run. That'd be an all-time record for me to claim.

• ○ ○ ◯ ○ ○ •

The Dragon Void didn't work out like I'd hoped. I heard some other Corellian won the whole thing, so I've got to raise my mug in their direction. That doesn't help me in the money department.

Looks like it's back to hauling for this spacer. Cargo, passengers, animals, I don't care. Give me a destination and I'll get there.

Need to find somebody to pay for my services. Thought about Tatooine, but remembered that they water down the drinks at Chalmun's. My next thought was Takodana.

I hope she appreciates that it's me bringing this book back into her possession. I hope she sees how I really feel.

MAZ KANATA

Little storyteller, how is it that you returned to me so early?

I foresaw a tangled track, one that far exceeded its journey thus far. I have cast a bottle into the ocean only for it to wash up at my feet. Surely the fault lies with me, not with the Force. I did not heave it into the proper current. Look who returned it to me, after all.

This book needs a stronger hand to carry it, and I know just the Wookiee.

> At least Chewie's not the only sucker who's gotten hooked. —Han

CHEWIE KEPT YAMMERING AT ME ABOUT THIS THING.

But I knew where he got it, and the big guy's a softy to any face that takes a shine to his blue eyes. I know how you feel, buddy, but don't let this logbook get you into hot water back on Kashyyyk.

Looks like this thing was Maz Kanata's way of tossing her wealth to any star hauler who's willing to pick up the trail. Could make some sucker very, very rich, if it doesn't wind up in the hands of the syndicates.

But Chewie and me, we own it now. Happy landings for a couple of freighter bums!

We've got a ship and a droid brain to steer her by, and as captain of this operation I've decided to go after Maz's hidden data node on Columi. Not much Hutt influence in that part of space. I like our odds.

Can't wait till Lando finds out. —Sana

Blasted out of Columi with a hull crack so deep it nearly split the *Falcon* in half when we jumped the Big L. Lucky I convinced my favorite outlaw techs to give me a discount on a spaceframe weld for no money down.

No, we didn't recover the data node. When did the Columi get so trigger-happy?

Now I've gotta dig out from under this debt, and a Wookiee for a partner is the last thing I need.

My old buddy Sonnoid introduced us to Mama Annie: a nice old lady and a custom spice chemist. I know better than to stick my neck out for anyone in this business, gray-haired sweetheart or no. Chewie? Don't get me started.

He overheard that Crymorah's Tantel mercs have been shaking down Mama, and now he thinks he's gotta be a hero. Chewie waited until the mercs finished raiding her money-changing office and ambushed them on their way to deposit it in their Bank of Coruscant numbered account.

Of course, I went along with it—what's the sense in my copilot getting skewered by metal-headed goons—but you'd better believe I had it out with Chewie about giving 90 percent of the haul back to Mama Annie. How's a guy supposed to make a living when his partner thinks everybody's a charity case?

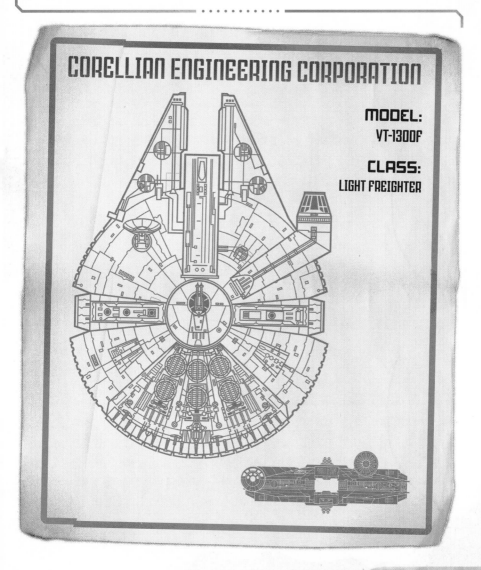

CORELLIAN ENGINEERING CORPORATION

MODEL:
YT-1300F

CLASS:
LIGHT FREIGHTER

Of all the gundark kissers who owned this book before me, why did one of 'em have to be Lando? The Force might be prime-grade bunkum, but the jury's still out on Lady Fate. If she's listening, this is some weak jet-juice. Look at what he wanted to do to my baby!

If a component doesn't help you fly or fight, it's not worth spending the credits. Yeah, I know what Lando would say, and he's wrong. The *Falcon*'s a fighter, just like me and Chewie. That's why I geared her up, so she could punch back at picket ships.

HAN SOLO'S MODS:

- **KDY SHIELD GENERATOR**: Military grade, so it's a good thing the Empire fell asleep when it came to guarding that weapons dump.
- **HANX-WARGEL SUPERFLOW IV COMMAND INTELLIGENCE**: No point in trying to compare the *Falcon*'s H-W to a stock model, not with L3 bouncing around in there. A little temperamental, but the best nav database anywhere.
- **HIDDEN ZX-108 "GROUND BUZZER" BLASTER CANNON**: Not really all that accurate, but good at scattering boarding parties and that's enough for me.
- **CARBANTI 29L COUNTERMEASURES PACKAGE AND SENSOR JAMMER**: Like Chewie says, if you can't run, you'd better be able to hide.
- **MY DICE**: First customization I ever made on this ship. It's more than just a lucky charm; it's also proof that I'm the better gambler.

NEED SOMETHING LIKE THIS FOR THE HEIST. HOW DID SOLO AFFORD ONE?
—LYLYED

You'd have thought the trick I pulled hauling coaxium out of Kessel would have made me famous. I tell the story to everybody, and everybody thinks I'm bluffing. But as Chewie is my witness: Han Solo made the Kessel Run in less than twelve parsecs!

You can keep your Kessel Run records. I don't care.

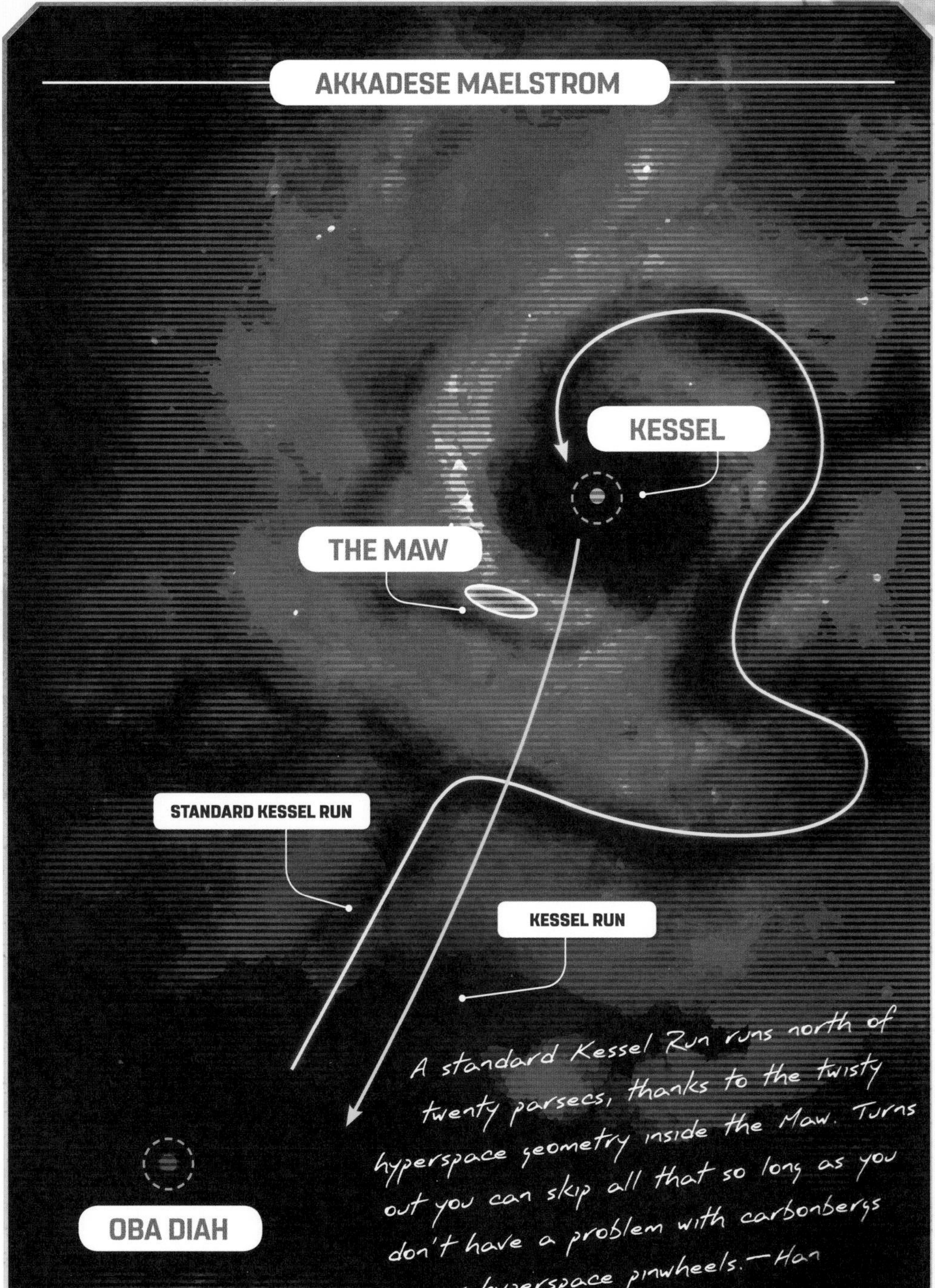

AKKADESE MAELSTROM

KESSEL

THE MAW

STANDARD KESSEL RUN

KESSEL RUN

OBA DIAH

A standard Kessel Run runs north of twenty parsecs, thanks to the twisty hyperspace geometry inside the Maw. Turns out you can skip all that so long as you don't have a problem with carbonbergs or hyperspace pinwheels. —Han

You know what, I do care! The nerve of these jet jockeys, laughing at me as soon as I turn my back.

I'm not bad with my fists, and good ol' Chewie's got a thing for arm-twisting. That guy on Junkfort bragging he did it in under eleven? Next time I'm out that way I'm gonna tell him to scratch gravel. I hope he throws a punch instead.

Looks like Crymorah came down pretty hard on Mama Annie. Chewie and me haven't felt any heat from the syndicates just yet, but in the meantime, I lined up a new client.

Got a job with Big Bunji running bogus authority cash vouchers to the rubes on the far side of the Cron Drift. I know that "smuggler's honor" says don't exploit anyone poorer than yourself. But we're running ragged, and we can't afford to start playing by the rules.

*Han, you're even crazier than you look.
—Sana*

Planning to mask the *Falcon*'s ID as *Graphite Skipper* for the job, just as soon as I can get Chewie to update the transponder.

Lots of Mining Guild TIEs in the Cron Belt, but Chewie and me can take 'em out with the quad cannons.

Yeah yeah, I know, buddy. Chewie says to write down that if either of us notches a kill in the Money Zone—the space around the *Falcon*'s perimeter reachable by both cannons—then it's worth double points. It's not like I'm worried. I'm ahead by three and he'd better not forget it.

Made a clean break with Bunji after the Cron scam, only to wind up in the decaying orbit of the galaxy's cheapest swindlers—the Briil Twins.

It's a simple run. Stash a couple hundred bottles of R'alla mineral water in the *Falcon*'s floor compartments, then smuggle the contraband to the clean-living people of Rampa II.

Setting the *Falcon*'s transponder to *Sunfighter Franchise* for this one. Hopefully we'll earn enough to get us off the Red List and shake the debt collectors.

RAMPA II PORT AUTHORITY
MERCHANDISE CLAIM FORM

IDENTITY OF PRISONER:

Solo, Han

IDENTITY OF CLAIMANT:

Starros, Sana

DETAILS OF CLAIM:

Claimant purports to be felon's wife, and therefore entitled to personal effects seized during "Rampa Rapids" smuggling intercept on 4237.4.
Claim approved by Agent 373–CR, Port Hoshim, Rampa II.

Well, "partner," looks like the cosmic deck dealt you a dead hand this time. I expect you're getting used to that by now. Too bad about Chewbacca, though. Wookiees deserve to have more say in who winds up on the receiving end of a life debt.

With Solo and Chewie in lockup on Rampa, it was pretty easy to slip the customs agent some creds and nab Solo's gear. I figure it's the least he owed me after he sold me out during that nerf-legging scam in the Monsua Nebula.

This logbook looks like it'll more than offset my expenses, what with this talk of treasure coordinates and data caches. When it comes to digging up buried riches, I know just the girl. Yeah, she's burned me before, too. But Aphra has got to be a better partner than Han-kriffing Solo.

I MEAN, AGREED?
STILL MAD, THOUGH.
—APHRA

PAPA TOREN

GRAKKUS JAHIBAKTI TINGI

"These Proofs of Prestige and Admiration are Bestowed Upon Grakkus the Hutt in Concordance with the Honored Customs of Syndicate Exchange by Which Our Grand Enterprises May Maintain an Accord of Mutual Benefit."

IN THE NAME OF PAPA TOREN, OF THE CASTELL CABAL AND WHISPER NETWORK, MAY THESE GIFTS SERVE GRAKKUS WELL:

» 1 VINTAGE LOGBOOK ONCE OWNED BY MAZ KANATA THE USURPER (SEIZED FROM AN INSOLENT SMUGGLER FOR NONPAYMENT OF PROTECTION FEES)

» 1 MODIFIED MARK VII GLADIATOR DROID, "STABINATOR" (15 CLEAN KILLS ON THE WUMPO CIRCUIT USING A POWER LANCE, A SUREFIRE CROWD-PLEASER!)

» 1 CONTRACT FOR THE SERVICES OF PLOOVO TWO-FOR-ONE, PAPA TOREN'S LONGSTANDING SHADOW BROKER FOR THE CORPSEC AND TION (BRINGS WITH HIM THOUSANDS OF CONTACTS, WHICH SHOULD HELP OPEN THE NILGAARD SECTOR FOR BUSINESS)

» 3 CASES OF JELLIED PANNA FROGS STEWED IN BLOODFRUIT BRINE (PAPA KNOWS THAT GRAKKUS HAS A SWEET TOOTH)

THIS PRIMECYCLE!
IT'S PIT FIGHT NIGHT!

THE MAIN EVENT

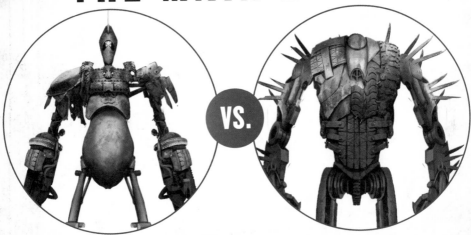

VS.

RHEEN THE POWDERIZER VS. SALLOWPINK
ENHANCED, ALL WEAPON MODS LEGAL!

GLADIATOR DROID DEVASTATION!

UNDERCARD MATC

OIL SPILLER VS. STABIN
SILICATE UPPERCUT VS. OVE

GRAKKUS ARENA, HUTTA TO
FRONT ROW "BLOOD ZONE": 2,500 CREDITS / ALL O

Mighty Grakkus, behold the
final design for the next cycle's
pit fight. Between ticket sales,
holonet views, and gambling, your
illustriousness will surely double
his wealth.

Chewie's got plenty to say about these guys. Nothing I want to repeat. —Han

XONTI BROTHERS

THE GALAXY'S PREMIER GLADIATOR TRAINERS

RECEIPT FOR DELIVERY OF MERCHANDISE

CLIENT: Grakkus the Hutt
PRODUCT: 3 fighters from Kashyyyk Group B9

- **"One-Eyed Volant"**
  Prime specimen, Ultraheavy Enhanced Class

- **"Ballast Breaker"**
  Mid-grade specimen, Heavyweight Grappler
  Class

- **"Snarrl the Feral"**
  Feeder specimen, Bantamweight Freestyle
  Class

MERCHANDISE HAS BEEN CERTIFIED DISEASE-FREE BY THE TRANDOSHAN PORT AUTHORITY

THIS VONTOR'S EVE, ENJOY A LIMITED ENGAGEMENT AT GRAKKUS ARENA . . .

BEAST FIGHTS!

GUNDARKS VS. NEXUS
NEKS VS. GARAGONS
SHRATS VS. SALKY HOUNDS

Mighty Grakkus: A thousand apologies for sharing this unfinished work, but we seek your wisdom on which matches the arena should host during the offseason.

ARENA FLOOR WILL BE FLOODED FOR A BATTLE ROYALE:
SAKES VERSUS THE HOUSE'S BATTLE-SCARRED ACKLAY,
OLD HARDSHELL.
PLACE YOUR BETS!

OF COURSE, MURRO THE FATHIER MINCES THE MARGENGAI GLIDE!
Between rounds, attendees can scale a greased ramp to claim an authentic Gallinore gem,
but beware—shredder blades will consume the laggards.

*What do they do with
the severed limbs? Ponda, find out!*
—Dr. Evazan

Mighty Grakkus, your oddsmakers wish to suggest how gamblers may be further exploited for the maximization of profits.

Ordering one of our competitors to take a fall is a potentially lucrative form of match fixing, but there is also money to be made by directing which fighter will draw first blood and with which weapon—as long as the house beats the point spread.

No governing body can censure us, and the gamblers in Hutta Town are a notoriously stupid lot.

Mighty Grakkus: As you know, the anticipated shipment of Mark X Executioner droids never arrived, despite the assurances of the thrice-cursed Latts Razzi. I trust that one of the following will meet with your approval instead.

• WED "Red Hell" Treadwell

• KO-5D modified general purpose droid "Maximo"

• Power Droid WG-22 "Gonk Gladiator"

NOTE FROM MARKETING:
In light of the growing popularity of our competition on Loovria, it is recommended to spend a quarter of this cycle's promotional budget on Cynabar's Infonet, specifically their sports coverage.

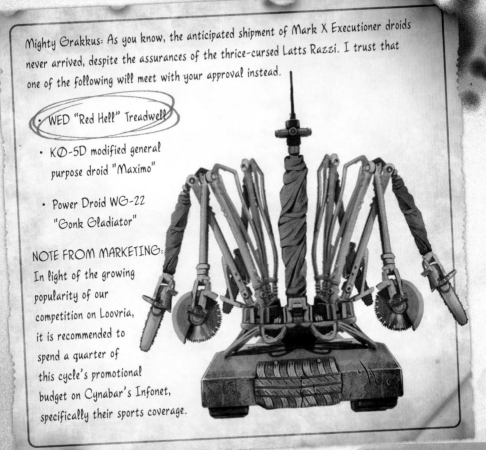

THIS CYCLE! JUNGLE FURY MEETS SURVIVOR'S RAGE! WHO WILL TRIUMPH?

ULTIMATE DEATH MATCH

FOR REVIEW ONLY
NOT ACTUAL SIZE

Mighty Grakkus:
As we approach the next
cycleshift, may this poster
that celebrates the upcoming
fatalities receive your favor.

ONE-EYED VOLANT THE EVISCERATOR VS. ZANDARREO, JETSAM OF LASAN

UNDERCARD MATCHES: METAL MAYHEM!

"RED HELL" TREADWELL VS. SILICATE UPPERCUT
B1 BEATDOWN VS. HEEP SPLITLING
MANDALORIAN BATTLE HARNESS FREE-FOR-ALL

GRAKKUS ARENA, HUTTA TOWN

THIS CYCLE! JUNGLE FURY MEI

ULTIMAT

~~ONE-EYED VOLANT
THE EVISCERATOR~~

NO. WROLLANPPF.

MISTRESS WROLLANPPF WISHES ME TO RECORD THE CIRCUMSTANCES OF HER GLADIATORIAL TRIUMPH USING THE LANGUAGE OF GALACTIC BASIC, TO WHICH SHE IS UNACCUSTOMED.

DURING THE LONG MONTHS THAT FOLLOWED HER ARRIVAL AT GRAKKUS ARENA, MISTRESS WROLLANPPF WORKED TIRELESSLY TO FORGE BONDS OF COMMON CAUSE AMONG THE GLADIATORS, ROUSTABOUTS, BEAST HANDLERS, AND STABLE SWEEPERS. FOR ARE WE NOT ALL UNITED IN OPPRESSION, NO MATTER THE CIRCUMSTANCES OF OUR BIRTH OR MANUFACTURE?

AND THUS, AT THE CLANGING OF THE BELL TO OPEN THE ARENA'S 7,072ND DEATH MATCH, MISTRESS WROLLANPPF RESPONDED WITH A ROAR THAT BEGAN THE ARENA'S FIRST SLAVE UPRISING.

   —STABINATOR, FORMER MARK VII GLADIATOR DROID, NOW MANUMITTED

Fikkesstarrl
HAKKARNUN-KURN
ᚦᚨᚾᚾᚢᚦᚦᚢᚨᚾᚾ ᚴᛖᚢ ᚦᚢᛁᚦ

Wotabarr
Little Yppysshyk

Chewie's been carrying this logbook around for months, and he never said a word! "Didn't think you'd be interested," he tells me.

I don't want to know the odds of this thing landing back in my hands like this, but I've seen longshots play out before. Chewie tells me a bunch of Wookiee warriors were passing it around, and he accepted it from Big Quince's bodyguard during that weapons trade on Orelon.

Ha—I KNEW it was Sana who robbed me back on Rampa! Chewie said no, but who was right, fuzzball? Who was right?

Kind of funny seeing your own words locked in time like that. It's almost hard to remember that hungry spell between Beckett and Jabba, but we ain't exactly lounging around on a Corellian pleasure yacht now.

We're still running with the Rebels. Most of 'em are okay. Luke's a good kid. I'd hire him on in a flash. Leia . . . she's got a lot to learn. Maybe some sucker'll put up

ALLIANCE TO RESTORE THE REPUBLIC
INTAKE AND PROCESSING FORM

NAME:
Chewbacca

AGE:
Unverified

HEIGHT:
2.28 meters

WEIGHT:
112 kilograms

OCCUPATION:
Freighter first mate

KNOWN ALIASES:
Greyfoul, Kiiruuk the Unbowed

PILOTING EXPERTISE:
Light freighters

COMMAND EXPERIENCE:
Kachirho Wookiee Militia
(see Clone Wars addendum)

with her long enough to make it stick, but it won't be me. I'm smart enough to steer clear of hassles like that.

THESE STONE-MUNCHERS ARE AN ARCHAEOLOGIST'S WORST ENEMY. —APHRA

Chewie's been digging these stone mites out of every nook and cranny inside the *Falcon*. Spent hours patching up their bite tracks and now I've got duracrete grout all over my shirt. Why don't we have a laundry aboard this ship? Constantly operating a few hundred thousand credits in the red is the kind of thing that gets in the way of clean living in ways you'd never expect.

My mind's made up. There's no money in the Rebellion and no security worth a damn. I've got enough death marks on my head without inviting even more from the Empire.

Chewie's too sweet to say it, but we can't afford to be sticking around here anymore. It's time this captain took his ship far away from here.

Honestly, Maz's logbook couldn't have shown up at a better time. If we get one of these treasures we can wipe out our debt and split any profits.

An uninspired dejarik maneuver, but perhaps a mathematical clue?
—Master Codebreaker

Oh, so now you want to add to this log? What kind of strategy is this? Bad move, buddy. I don't know what you're hiding inside that furry dome of yours. You make that move, the glory's all mine.

Don't rub it in, pal. No one likes a smug winner. You're just tempting fate with this winning streak of yours.

Decided to go after one of Maz's tougher prizes: the *Graceful Promising*, a derelict Vontorian treasure ship locked in close orbit around a dark star.

I know what you're thinking: there's not a freighter bum alive who'd risk that much gravitational shear. Good thing I'm the only pilot who's ever notched a sub-12 Kessel Run.

Bringing Lieutenant Ematt and a couple of Alliance Pathfinders too. They're pretty good in a fight as rebels go, and Chewie and me might need some extra hands aboard the *Falcon*.

Not a bad bit of treasure hauling from the *Grateful Promising*, if I do say so myself. Lucky for Ematt that I was able to find a buyer for all that kiirium.

WISH I'D GOTTEN THE FIRST CRACK AT
IT. I KNOW A FEW TECHNIQUES.
—CYCYED OCK

They needed the money so I let them keep most of it, to maybe buy another ion cannon or something. That leaves Chewie and me playing catch-up, though. How come a guy like me can never catch a break?

Got to plan a new job for paying down Jabba's loan. Not sharing it with sad-sack Rebels this time.

Possible clients:

The Ezaraa? Religious types always promise big credits, but these guys actually paid up when we came to collect. Problem is, I'm pretty sure they still have us marked as heretics in their holy texts. But the way I see it, if they didn't want us to laugh at that old guy, they shouldn't have made his hat so tall. Right, Chewie?

The Aquaris Freeholders? Chewie won't stop dropping hints about linking back up with this outfit even though they once hijacked our spice cargo. I'm starting to think that Silver Fyre must have cooed in his ear about his big blue eyes.

We don't have a job lined up, but I'm plotting a course for the Bright Jewel Cluster anyway. Thinking we can jostle some elbows on Tansarri Point. Maybe even pay a visit to Ord Mantell if we don't see any hostile chatter on the Undervine.

Or maybe we'll go there anyway. Big risks bring big payouts, and Han Solo ain't scared of anything.

SHESSLARIA,
LICENSED SKIP TRACER

MEMBERSHIPS:

INTERSTELLAR COLLECTIONS
LIMITED, BOUNTY HUNTERS
GUILD (CREDIT RECOVERY
DIVISION)

UNDERVINE NULLSTRING:
049X88108

TRANSCRIBED DATA [BEGIN]

DAYS TO PAYOUT: 7

One day's distance from Ord Mantell in my rearview, but it'll be at least a week until I reach Zorba's palace in the Southern Rim. Hate using untraveled hyperlanes, but I can't be sure a hunt saboteur didn't pick up my vector. Better to keep things slow and steady until I make delivery.

I can fill my time with making mark in this log. Strange how I got my hands on it. Probably some kind of bounty bust that went bad. Picked this up and split before anybody noticed me. Don't know who the target was. Probably this Han Solo guy.

Never heard of him. Though by what he wrote, I'm not surprised things went south.

DAYS TO PAYOUT: 5

Checked on my cargo. He's still breathing. Get this, he asked if I'd crank up the air recirculators. Gave me my first laugh in ages. Buddy, I would if I could!

Hey, if he wanted to live his life in comfort, he shouldn't have taken out a loan from a Hutt. It's his debt, not mine. I'm just the agent who makes sure he pays it in person.

DAYS TO PAYOUT: 3

Arm still burns. Can't believe I let that dinko-lover graze me with a needlebeamer before I grabbed him.

The bandage is starting to turn green but I'm too scared to unwrap it. The stink would probably knock me flat.

DAYS TO PAYOUT: 1

This sticky, recycled atmo aboard this ship, it isn't helping my arm one bit. But I keep reminding myself that's what Zorba's fee is for.

Fix the recirculator. Fix my arm. Fix my whole skrogging life while I'm at it.

Making a quick stop at Jedha to recalibrate my navicomputer, then it's a straight shot to payday.

TRANSCRIBED DATA [END]

Pathetic that a skip tracer should bring me so low! Everyone hates the bill collector—everyone except destiny, it seems.

The target that she carried, he had rich friends. They cared enough to hire a hunt saboteur like me, so that I could interrupt her delivery and save that man from the cruelties of the Hutts. They could have just given him the money to pay off the debt in the first place, and I would have never gotten involved! It seems their caring was conditional.

It matters not. In this moment, no one cares for me. The crash landing snapped my starboard foil and my physiology won't last long under this desert sun. It seems that I will die in the dust.

My name is Puttana Pin. Witness me, for once I was a life.

Back when I threw my lot in with the Partisans, that was a right steady gig for old Cycyed Ock. No, I was never much of a zealot, but I was savvy enough to say the right things.

Saw Gerrera—rest his bones—wasn't the worst commander I ever had. But sometimes he'd get that wild blaze in his stare. When that happened, I'd start screaming for the Emperor's head louder than anyone else in the room—because if I didn't, Gerrera might've started screaming for my head too.

Me and Kullbee, we're the only survivors of Gerrera's Partisans with any brains. We relocated to the other hemisphere after the Empire took a bite out of the planet, but it's all red powder wherever you go.

Ran across a crashed Headhunter the other day—one of the old suicide sleds, with a couple blaster holes in its fuselage—and lifted this logbook from the sunburned blubber of whatever used to be its pilot. Now I'm interested! —Evazan

Smart move. Because buried treasure and encrypted data nodes sound like money to me. It's time to get the old gang back together.

Kullbee, bless his braids, already said yes.

So from what I can tell, one of Maz's treasure hauls has almost certainly gone unclaimed. I think I've figured out where she hid it and I'd have probably done the same thing.

Cities on Iskalon, a waterworld, rely on plasma that's pumped directly from the ocean floor. Maz's treasure? It's inside one of those pipelines. Can't detect it from the outside thanks to energy interference, and can't reach it from the inside with that much fluidic pressure.

Now, maybe you could cause a plasma spill on purpose. But who'd be able to swoop in, at those depths, and make off with the treasure in serpent-infested waters, and all before the automated sentinels sealed the breach?

A ragtag team of oddballs, that's who. Let me pull up that Imperial alert from way back . . .

To all captains of interstellar commerce vessels, welcome to the historic Terrabe sector. Be advised that bandit activity is on the rise. You are part of the solution. If you notice anything suspicious, report it!

In particular, stay alert for the following members of the so-called Gullet Gang:

1. **CYCYED OCK, KEREDIAN CYBORG SHARPSHOOTER**

   Left Gallandro's old gang but broke a contract with the Droid Gotra; was forced to outdraw a succession of mechanical duelists and shot dead by #11

2. **NERSITON, SINITEEN INFO BROKER AND DATA SLICER**

3. **KULLBEE SPERADO, MEFTIAN GUNSLINGER**

4. **OOS-RIN-ARREK, TISS-SHAR CONTORTIONIST**

   Last seen with Gar Jan Rue's Traveling Menagerie; no way to contact her in time

5. **ISIN, ADVOZSEC FINANCIER AND BRAWLER**

6. **RUFORK "SHARP TOOTH" TAMSON, KARKARODON STUNT RACER**

   Joined the Mon Cal opera players but injured a fin during performance of "The Neka-Chisler"

Too many holes in the old gang.

Time to start recruiting a new gang. That's the thing they never tell you about oddballs: being unique doesn't mean you can't be replaced.

ATTACHMENT: ISHALON_FACILITY_2235DA

Ishalon's pump station #2235DA is 3,121.7m below sea level. Have entered this into my calculations. — Master Codebreaker

Kullbee says he likes my replacement crew. And he was even willing to go so far as to tell me that he likes our odds.

Wish I felt the same. Too much Imperial attention in that neck of the galaxy, and the syndicates take a dim view of independent operators like us.

IMPERIAL BUREAU OF PUNITIVE CORRECTION

MEGALOX BETA PENITENTIARY
ᒫᐅᑊᕐᐳᐊ ᔑᐱᑊᕐ ᑭᐱᐊᑲᐴ ᕓᐊᑊᐅᑫᖑᐴ

This pronouncement issued by:
Rehabilitation officer Sam Kenzie

Got close to the leader of the new inmates. It's like I thought. They DID steal that treasure on Iskalon, and only got collared after they stashed it somewhere. All that stuff from the pipeline owners about a sickened mega eel crashing the pipeline and causing the breach? Just a cover-up for investors.

The Keredian promises that if I spring his whole crew, he'll cut me in for a quarter share.

Need to grab his logbook out of the Personal Property Annex first, which sounds like it's a map leading to more targets like that one. After that, it's jailbreak time.

So long, Megalox. I've always hated this job.

WARNING: ALL TRANSMITTABLE COMMUNICATIONS MUST BE REVIEWED BY PENITENTIARY SECURITY PRIOR TO DISSEMINATION

GALACTIC WHISPER NETWORK,
OPTIMIZATION STRAND

INFO BROKER 2757:

WESSEX, PRIMA

When one visits a tavern, if one should encounter a patron who loudly proclaims his intention to pay for the drinks of everyone present—well, that is a sign that said patron has come into sudden wealth. One can recognize such an obvious fact without belonging to the info broker profession.

However, we info brokers are unique among the galaxy's underworld players in our ability to resist free-flowing Hedrett whiskey. It is very likely,

122

therefore, that I was the only being on all of Hosnian Prime with the presence of mind to steal the source of the red-faced man's power during the peak of his cognitive befuddlement.

Farewell, Mr. Kenzie. This artifact briefly brought you good fortune but is now in more capable hands.

For now that the Whisper Network possesses an item with such a high potential value, logic dictates three actions:

- ONE, that this logbook undergo multiple methods of independent authentication to verify its origins;

- TWO, that a sampling of high-value targets (Pashvi, Moldour 14, and Seylott, for example) be visited by trained investigators to determine whether they still house intact treasures (or, if not, that they have been disturbed in a manner consistent with the narratives recorded in this logbook);

- THREE—and only upon confirmation of points one and two—that the information in this logbook be copied into discrete units of comparable value and sold off to underworld buyers.

The Whisper Network keeps the galactic underworld running. With the information in this artifact, we will steer the syndicates along vectors of our choosing. It has always been thus. It will always be so.

Deep Current? The Assemblers? In their limited vision they are beneath our notice. The Kupohan Spynet? Don't make me laugh.

No one ever sees the Whisper Network, but our info brokers are everywhere, and we are always three moves ahead.

LOG ENTRY: EXULTATION

Oh Ponda, what a spectacle! For someone like me to receive an invitation to the Obroan Intelligence Summit, that is a true honor. And that I took the invitation from a disemboweled and former info broker—that is a testament to the ingenuity of Dr. Evazan!

How clever of me to peel the agent's skin and fool the door scanner outside Obroa-skai's Stratosphere Room. Surely those in attendance should be applauding in delighted surprise. Don't you agree?

What a shame, then, that you and I cannot hear their applause in a room furnished with bodies and carpeted with an expanding spill of redness. Ponda, I admire those who trade in information, I do. But some beings—gods, really—trade in life and death itself!

It is true that I consider myself an architect of the vital arts. I despise cloners—obedient clerks, all of them—as well as the so-called cryptosurgeons who think a job title is a shortcut to genius.

Should we begin, my beloved Ponda? Our materials are all around us. Such an excess of limbs and viscera, and from so many species! We will load them on the ship.

LOG ENTRY: PUZZLEMENT

After fourteen days, not even a murmur concerning the Obroa-skai massacre? I suppose if you kill the info brokers, no one is left to spread the news. I'm a little disappointed at getting away with it so easily, Ponda.

I know what you will say. "You already have the death sentence in twenty-two systems. Who cares about one more?" I appreciate that, my friend.

LOG ENTRY: WISTFULNESS

Ponda, your tusks will quiver when I tell you this bittersweet tale.

Long ago, in the Kingdom of the Tion, a dying princess taught her pipe-bird to whistle her favorite song. Other birds learned to mimic the same pattern of notes, and throughout thousands of years of spaceflight, they spread across the galaxy. Think

BUILDING A BETTER BEING!

GRAFT-RESISTANT

PROMISING!

TOO EASY

POSSIBLE ALLERGENS

of it, Ponda. Every time you've heard a pipe-bird, a princess has sung to you from beyond the grave.

That is what I seek! Immortality! These wretches I build are the means to unlocking the galaxy's greatest secret.

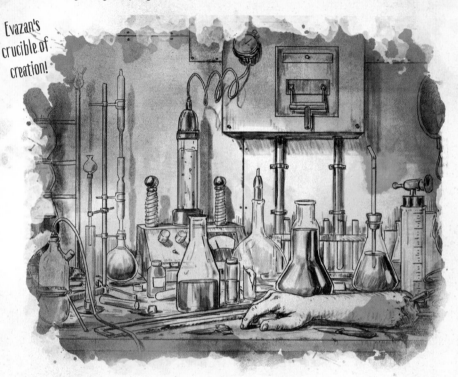

Evazan's crucible of creation!

LOG ENTRY: PERSISTENCE

Ponda, I've said this before, but that incident in the Tatooine cantina was quite a while ago. Why do you continue to resist?

A cyborg arm is out of the question. Do you want to look like some disposable pit fighter, with a razor-tipped gripper that also squirts acid? I care about you too much to consider such a circus of spectacle.

Some of the arms from the Stratosphere Room still haven't rotted. Just give me the word and one of them will be yours.

LOG ENTRY: INVENTIVENESS

I admire your resilience, Ponda. I know you have toiled to bring me credits. I recognize that shaking down shopkeepers is exhausting.

But what if I used all these credits to develop fresh poisons? We could test them in laced sweetcakes you could deliver to a nearby orphanage.

I'm bored, Ponda! Think what we could learn about toxicity!

LOG ENTRY: RUMINATION

My friend, give me your honest opinion of this verse.

> *For how could the cries of the victims be heard*
> *'Midst rebalanced humors and vitals transferred*
> *'Tis skill that defines noble Evazan's art*
> *As the throats of his victims shall one day impart*

Surprised, Ponda? How wonderful that, after so many years, we can still make new discoveries about each other.

LOG ENTRY: RESENTMENT

Surely you remember my disappointment at receiving no response to my application to join the Alchemists Guild? Now how do you think I reacted when I learned that the Alchemists Guild hasn't actually existed in nearly a millennium?

LOG ENTRY: CONTEMPLATION

I am remembering that time I spent on Athus Klee, shaping the perfect miner for the Crimson Dawn syndicate. Interesting work at the beginning but you know how quickly other minds drive me to boredom.

I am an artist, Ponda, not a contractor.

LOG ENTRY: URGENCY

The experiment has reached a critical stage! I need heads!

Ponda, I'm out of bone powder! Dig up a dozen corpses, preferably ones that have marinated for at least three centuries. Makem Te has an entire landmass of well-labeled graves. Whatever we don't use we'll grind up and sell to the elixir hustlers on Nar Shaddaa.

LOG ENTRY: EXULTATION

We've done it again, Ponda. Another original. We have built new life!

But . . . too many arms? I could remove one of the ones in the back and have it grafted to your stump in no time. Just let me know that you agree.

I'm a proud parent! Go make friends, my offspring!

That thing that was carrying this, I put a blaster bolt clean through its head. Was that its head? Don't know, don't care.

But it's like I told my uncle, I ain't a bad shot! "Anton Markox: soldier of fortune." Don't hate it, I guess.

So where's the nearest crime boss who's looking for a hired gun?

For many generations, those of the Pavel-Martinus lineage have been courtesans, serving at the pleasure of an Exalted Hutt or a syndicate's Grand Dynast and excelling in the arts of idleness, indulgence, and flattery.

And yet, my secret shame is that the investment has begun to outweigh the gains. When I was accepted into the court of Buggine the Hutt, I preened in jubilation, for her style of extravagant frivolity has been in rare supply since the downfall of Ziro. Keeping pace with her other courtesans has required the purchase of velvet capes, silver slippers, vinegar-oil perfumes, and even gilt-inlayed grog goblets.

Why, just yesterday I appeared at court resplendent in rainbow gems, only to discover that Buggine had decreed feathered epaulets to be this cycle's hottest fashion. How will I afford such whimsies? Pompey Pavel-Martinus will be ruined!

How refreshing that you, dear diary, are no hissing gossip.

DOK-ONDAR'S
DEN OF ANTIQUITIES

ITEM DESCRIPTION

Used spacer's logbook obtained from criminal fence.
Colorful history of ownership. Might be fake.

SELL IN SHOP

_ _ _ _ YES

_ _ _ _ NO

SUGGESTED PRICE

_ _ _ _ _ _ _

Haven't made up my mind about this yet. Going to ship it to
the Core so that Sava Fissis Fen of the University of Bar'leth
can take a look. Might wind up with a "VERIFIED: BAR'LETH
ANTIQUITIES" sticker, which usually triples the selling price.

IIAE

IMPERIAL INSTITUTE FOR ARCHAEOLOGICAL EXPLOITATION

THULE, ESSTRAN SECTOR

NAME:
Dr. Chelli Lona Aphra

ACCREDITATIONS:
University of Bar'leth, Archaeological Association of Archaeo-Prime, University of Rudrig Committee for Historic Preservation

The bearer of this certificate has limited clearance to access sites of historical interest to the Empire, pursuant to bylaws 22.750–23.018 of the Harvester Accords

This must've been what Sana was talking about during that drink-off at Fort Ypso. Most people who ingest that much *aquae infurnus* start babbling nonsense, but looks like Sana surprised me again.

All these idiots who've owned this logbook, and I'm the first accredited archaeologist. So to them I say: Great job, boys, you really mucked up some historic sites. It's a straight-up cultural tragedy.

Before I start poking around these sites myself, I want to take a look into a deeper pattern. Maz's treasures looked pretty evenly spaced across the civilized galaxy, but the ones that have been claimed so far seem to have benefited the syndicates in the Eastern Rim. Just a hunch, but it might explain why Crimson Dawn and Crymorah are losing ground while the Hutts and the Pykes are consolidating assets.

Is that what you're up to, little book? Destabilizing the underworld balance of power?

Figure I might check out Descopose Farmark first. It's in the back end of Wild Space, practically in the Unknown Regions. Nobody seems to care about the backscatter boonies.

IMPOUNDED IN THE NAME OF SUPREME LEADER SNOKE OF THE FIRST ORDER

ASSET SEIZURE APPROVED BY:
COMMANDANT BRENDOL HUX

I thought the Irving Boys brought me on for an apprenticeship, but I guess not! Not when they dumped me at the last wayfarers' node. Well, blanks to them. They gave me this "onboarding pack" and I'm keeping it. It's decent stuff for getting started as a smuggler:

- » Waterproof poncho that doubles as a rain catcher
- » Hyperspace sextant
- » Huttese phrase book (looks like a bunch of pages have been ripped out)
- » Fake piloting license template
- » Spice purity testing kit
- » Insulated bedroll that only deploys through facial recognition? No idea why, and I hate the image it stored.

DEVARONIAN EXPLORERS STARSCATTER BEDROLL, MODEL #K26957

Moisture-resistant gaberwool insulation rated for Class 3 environments and above

PRERECORDED FACIAL IMAGERY:

RILEY

Thermal comfort to be provided upon successful mapping of cranial contours

Also, for some reason, the pack included this logbook. Maybe they forgot where they put it?

Cybernetics are such a pain.

Look at this: the 66K needs a novic patellar to power the joint, but BioTech only sells it in the Core and Colonies. So I'm using a Lotho Junker omnislug instead, which means I've got to manually reroute the limbic impulses. Which is pretty much just me banging on my thigh every half hour, like some penitent cultist.

It doesn't matter if the Irving Boys ditched me. I've always been able to steal whatever I need. But things look different now that Palpatine's been wiped. Everybody always said the Empire would fold without an Emperor, but they seem like they're digging in on Burnin Konn and other worlds. That's why I wanted to hook up with people who had connections, and look where that got me.

Who knows where the Irving Boys got this logbook in the first place? We met up in the Anoat sector, but they could've come from the Southern Reaches, maybe even the Unknown Regions.

Nothing to steal out there anyway. See ya, dummies!

I've got a plan on what to do next. I've worked with the Ivax syndicate before. I know they're a feeder network for the Red Key Raiders. Those guys cut the guts out of the Hutt syndicate after Jabba's death on Tatooine. Wish I could've been there. I'd have given a wink to whichever syndicate assassin finally pulled the trigger on that slime-tracking slug.

An underworld restructure sounds like the perfect time for someone like me to make a little money. There's a Gabdorin who came to Burnin Konn once in a while to get a brine-soaking. Quiggold, I think? If he's not running with the Red Key Raiders, I bet he knows somebody who is.

Pretty big upgrade from the South Sector Sinners, but there's never been a better time for me to make a new beginning.

Sure, I told her, we need deckhands, but I could throw a rock and hit a dozen seasoned spacers in this cantina alone. And every one of 'em's got enough brains to leave "thief" off a list of job qualifications!

But I didn't hate her or nothing, so I recommended her to the Gray Gundarks as a swabbie crewer. Better them taking the risk than us, I figured. And all it cost her was the stuff in this satchel. I'd spotted the sextant, but turns out it's busted. Nearly tossed the whole bag but now I'm mighty glad I didn't.

Cap'n's gonna love this logbook. No bigger fan o' pirate lore than him, and sure as skating that's Gunda Mabin's script logging her pursuit of the treasures of Maz Kanata. Two Pirate Queens! And with this thing guiding

our way, we just might end up enthroning a new Pirate King.

Doubt he'd like that title, though—not hardly specific enough. Nobody ever forgets his painted Kaleesh mask, so we've been trying out Blood Buccaneer. Red Raider was my idea, but on most days Cap'n is preferrin' Crimson Corsair.

That skinny thief was wrong about me belongin' to the Red Key Raiders, but I can see how she'd think that given how much the cap'n favors that color scheme.

It's gonna take a lot of victories for us to write our own legend. Here's what we need to build on.

For hire!

Meson Martinet

CAPTAIN: Sidon Ithano, the Crimson Corsair
TERRITORY: Lost Clusters beyond the Outer Rim
BUSINESS: Piracy, privateering, raiding, banditry

DIRECT INQUIRIES TO:
First Mate Quiggold in the Ratoweel cantina,
Ponemah Terminal

Have entered hyperspatial compensatory
buffer coordinates into my calculations.
—Master Codebreaker

Sidon Ithano

Quiggold

Not my most flattering image. Keep meaning to shed those kilos. —Quiggold

Pendewqell

Reeg Brosna

Reveth

Squeaky

Chewie, is this the same guy we hired for the Fromm job? —Han

UNDERVINE NODE 137577

KEEP YOUR DISTANCE FROM THESE SWINDLERS, DESERTERS, AND BACKSTABBERS

Sidon Ithano, a diseased dinko who thinks loyalty isn't worth a saucer of Hutt spit, is now plying the Lost Clusters with a ship and crew. Be warned: he is a venom-barbed maggot. Ask him about his service aboard the New Gilliland—bet you 100 creds he won't answer. Ignore Ithano, and instead look up the freebooters wronged by his betrayal. Hire Captain Scorza and his Weequay gang!

That's true at least, but not for the reasons he's hinting at. The cap'n hardly ever talks to anybody, including his bleedin' first mate! —Quiggold

ANONYMOUS REFERRALS:
Use Undervine node 3375507.220, Kellux system

Scorza betrayed that ship to the Hutts so he could score some quick credits. It still burns him that the cap'n made it out of that debacle alive, and carrying enough plunder to start a gang of his own. —Quiggold

Just like I thought, the cap'n was all in when I showed him this log. This time tomorrow, Sidon Ithano's crew sets sail for the Lost Treasure of Adratharpe 7.

Sure as the *Martinet* attracts mynocks, we've picked up our share of rivals—and not just Scorza's boys. Things could get bloody if they're tracking us. I've never known the cap'n to back down from a fight.

UNDERBOSS, RED KEY RAIDERS

THE CRIMSON CORSAIR? HAH! MORE LIKE THE . . . RED . . . <u>IDIOT</u>!

WE SENT ITHANO AND HIS PANTOMIME PIRATES SCAMPERING LIKE LASH-CHASTENED NEKS.

FOUND THIS BOOK IN THE LAST HOVERCART ON ADRATHARPE. I KNEW RIGHT AWAY THAT BOSS MOVELLAN NEEDED TO SEE IT.

IT'S PLAIN THAT RED KEY'S PARTNERSHIP WITH BLACK SUN STILL CHAFES HIM. BOSS'LL GIVE A LISTEN TO ANYTHING THAT'LL LET US SHRUG OFF THE HAND OF THE OLD SYNDICATES. TIME TO LAY DOWN A NEW POWER STRUCTURE FOR THE POST-EMPIRE UNDERWORLD.

DROID GOTRA HAS ELIMINATED AN ARMED UBRIKKIAN FREIGHTER AT THE COORDINATES OF PERLEMIAN SPUR WAYPOINT 634BESH

DROID GOTRA HAS IDENTIFIED FREIGHTER'S ALLEGIANCE AS **RED KEY RAIDERS**

DROID GOTRA GAMMA-BIT 0001010000111000001111001 SWEPT THE WRECKAGE AND RETRIEVED THIS UNIQUE ASSEMBLAGE OF COMPRESSED WOOD PULP WITH STAMPED-INK INFORMATIONAL INDICATORS

THE ITEM'S CONTENTS HAVE BEEN TRANSLATED AND SCANNED WITH VALUABLE DATAPOINTS FLAGGED

DROID GOTRA SEEKS INFORMATIONAL ADVANTAGE; DROID GOTRA DOES NOT PURSUE MONETARY EXCESS

ALL AGENTS OF DROID GOTRA AND CYBAN FRONT SITUATED IN THE RIM TERRITORIES ARE TO TARGET THE CLOSEST DATA CACHE UPON RECEIPT OF BURST TRANSMISSION

```
01001011 01100001 01101100 01101100 01100101 01100001 00100000
01110011 01100101 01100011 01110100 01101111 01110010 00100000
01010100 01100101 01110010 01101101 01101001 01101110 01110101
01110011

01011001 01110101 01110011 01101000 01100001 01101110 00100000
01110011 01100101 01100011 01110100 01101111 01110010 00100000
01001100 01101001 01110100 01110100 01101100 01100101 00100000
01010000 01100101 01110100 01110010 01101111 01110110 01101001

01000011 01101111 01110010 01100010 01100101 01110100 01110100
00100000 01110011 01100101 01100011 01110100 01101111 01110010
00100000 01000011 01101111 01110010 01100010 01100101 01110100
01110100 00100000 01000011 01101100 01110101 01110011 01110100
01100101 01110010
```

> MACHINES CAN THINK, BUT CAN THEY REASON? DO THEY KNOW THE PULL OF INSTINCT? DO THEY HUNGER?

COMPARED TO KANJIKLUB'S SOFT BODIES, MAYBE THEY DO. BUT NOT TO THE GUAVIAN DEATH GANG. TO US, THEIR IMITATIVE CONSCIOUSNESS IS INFANTILE.

> NOW, WHAT SHOULD WE DO WITH THESE SPOILS OF BATTLE? HOW MIGHT THIS LOGBOOK GIVE US AN EDGE OVER OUR RIVALS?

THE TRIUMPH OF THE GUAVIAN DEATH GANG IS INEVITABLE. IT IS ONLY THE TIMETABLE THAT IS UNCERTAIN.

OUR SECURITY SOLDIERS ARE MACHINE-ENHANCED FROM CRANIUM TO EXTREMITIES. CHEMICAL PUMPS FEED THE ENDOCRINE SYSTEM TO BOOST RESPONSE TIME AND DULL PAIN RECEPTORS. CRANIAL FACEPLATES COLLECT

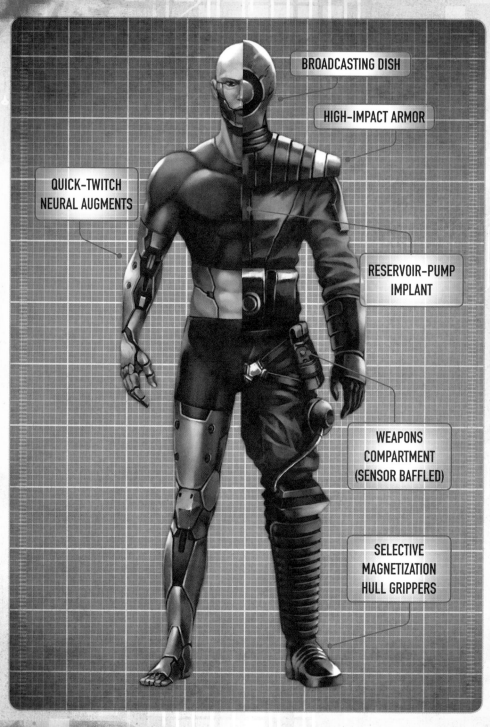

BROADCASTING DISH

HIGH-IMPACT ARMOR

QUICK-TWITCH
NEURAL AUGMENTS

RESERVOIR-PUMP
IMPLANT

WEAPONS
COMPARTMENT
(SENSOR BAFFLED)

SELECTIVE
MAGNETIZATION
HULL GRIPPERS

142

SIGNALS AND PERMIT NEAR-INSTANTA-
NEOUS COMMUNICATION ACROSS HYPER-
WAVE CHANNELS.

THIS IS THE FACE OF THE FUTURE. RUN
THE COMBAT ODDS IF YOU DOUBT ME.

> I, BALA-TIK, AM IN MY EARLY STAGE OF
MECHAMORPHOSIS AND POSSESS ONLY
ONE IMPLANT. BUT THE SILICATE GRAFTS
IN MY LEG ARE CLAMPED TO NERVE
ENDINGS, AND THIS ALONE IS SUFFICIENT
TO PROVIDE A QUICKDRAW EDGE OF 0.512
SECONDS MEASURED FROM THREAT
DETECTION TO FIRST-BURST. I DIDN'T
EVEN SPEC FOR THIS—MY BODY JUST
RESPONDED.

THE EMPIRE HAD LAWS AGAINST
CYBORG ENHANCEMENTS, BUT WHERE
IS THE EMPIRE NOW? THE SO-CALLED
NEW REPUBLIC IS TOOTHLESS, LACKING
THE FIREPOWER TO BACK UP ITS WORDS.
WITH NO ONE TO CHECK AMBITIONS,
IT IS THE GUAVIAN DEATH GANG WHO
WILL SET NEW STANDARDS FOR WHAT A
CONSCIOUS MIND CAN ACCOMPLISH.

> OUR SECURITY SOLDIERS ARE HALF
DROID, AND THEREFORE INTERCEPTING

*This guy. If you
loan money to
somebody,
you've gotta
give them time
to pay it off.
Kids these
days. —Han*

THE BINARY BURSTS SENT BY THE DROID
GOTRA PRESENTED NO DIFFICULTIES AT
ALL. WE QUICKLY IMPLEMENTED OUR
COUNTERACTION.

```
01000100 01110010 01101111 01101001 01100100 00100000
01000111 01101111 01110100 01110010 01100001 00100000
01110100 01101111 00100000 01110011 01110100 01110010
01101001 01101011 01100101 00100000 01101000 01101001
01100111 01101000 00101101 01111110 01100001 01101100
01110101 01100101 00100000 01110100 01100001 01110010
01100111 01100101 01110100 01110011 00100000 01101111
01101110 00100000 01010100 01100101 01110010 01101101
01101001 01101110 01110111 01110011 00100000 01001001
01101001 01110100 01110100 01101100 01100101 00100000
01010000 01100101 01110100 01110010 01101111 01101110
01101001 00100000 01100001 01101110 01100100 00100000
01000011 01101111 01110010 01110010 01100101 01110100
01110100 00100000 01000011 01101100 01110101 01110011
01110100 01100101 01110010

01010000 01101111 01110011 01101001 01110100 01101001
01101111 01101110 00100000 01110011 01101111 01101100
01100100 01101001 01100101 01110010 01110011 00100000
01100110 01101111 01110010 00100000 01101001 01101110
01110100 01100101 01110010 01100011 01100101 01110000
01110100 00001010
```

How enticing. —Master Codebreaker

THIS—ALL OF THIS—IS WHY THE
GUAVIAN DEATH GANG ARE DESTINED
TO SUPPLANT ORGANIC SWEAT LICKERS

LIKE THE KANJIKLUBBERS. FOR WHAT ARE THEY? FORMER SLAVES AND FAILED PIT FIGHTERS, ALL OF THEM INDISTIN-GUISHABLE FROM MONOTONE STREET TRASH.

> THE GUAVIAN DEATH GANG HAVE SET THEIR SIGHTS BEYOND KANJIKLUB. OUR NANO-PROPHETS HAVE COMPLETED THE ABSORPTION OF THE DATA THAT THE DROID GOTRA STOLE FROM KANATA'S REPOSITORIES, AND THAT DATA IS NOW OURS TO ACT UPON.

DOMINATION OF THE GALACTIC UNDER-WORLD BEGINS NOW, WITH A MASSIVE STRIKE ON NANTOON.

IT APPEARS THAT THE TIMETABLE OF THE TAKEOVER IS NO LONGER UNCERTAIN. OUR SECURITY SOLDIERS WILL LAUNCH THEIR ASSAULT FIVE CYCLES FROM THE TIME OF THIS MARK.

> FOUR CYCLES.

> THREE.

> TWO.

I AM RAZOO QIN-FEE. THE GUAVIAN DEATH GANG ARE STUPEFIED, THEIR NERVES STUNNED FROM THE FLURRY OF BLOWS LAUNCHED BY KANJIKLUB DURING THE SKIRMISH IN THE CRONESE MANDATE.

WE TOOK EVERYTHING FROM THOSE ZERO-SKULLS! WE TOOK SO MUCH THAT THE TRAIN OF FREIGHTERS STRETCHES ALL THE WAY BACK TO FORAN TUTHA, WITH EACH NEW CARGO OFFERED AT THE FEET OF TOPBOSS TASU LEECH.

GUAVIAN DEATH GANG SWALLOWS BITTER HUMILIATION!
YAMA KILLE CHESKAR GOO!
KANJIKLUB GRANDIO!

THEIR INFORMATION? WE WILL DECODE IT. THEIR INGOTS? WE WILL SPEND THEM!

WE WILL BURN ALL GUAVIANS INSIDE THEIR SHELLS!
E CHU TA, GUAVIAN!
NEE CHOO!

WE KANJIKLUBBERS FOUGHT AT CHASIDRON SHOALS. ANOTHER BOUT WHERE WE KNOCKED OUR CHALLENGERS STUPID.

WHO'S NEXT? BLACK SUN, THE CRYMORAH, CRIMSON DAWN? ANYBODY ELSE WHO USED TO THINK THEY RAN THE GALAXY?

THE OLD WAYS CAN'T STAND FOREVER. THE HUTTS ARE ALREADY SPIRALING INTO A CRASH. KANJIKLUB WILL MAKE SURE THERE ARE NO SURVIVORS!

THE TIME OF THE HUTTS HAS ENDED!
STY-UKA, SLEEMO!
WOMPITY DU WERMO!

TASU LEECH SAYS KANJIKLUB SHOULD WELD A BOND WITH THE WEAPONS MAKERS. THEY ARE THE GALAXY'S TRUE POWERS, AND THEY ARE SLOBBERING TO HOOK UP WITH KANJIKLUB.

WE WILL SET OFF TO CANTONICA IN THE MORNING. KANJIKLUB WILL STAND AT CENTER RING, FISTS WRAPPED!

ME JUUS KU!
BOSKA, PATEESA!
KANJIKLUB GRANDIO!

az Kanata, you are as charming as ever. This is your most inspired move to date.

I have enjoyed our back-and-forth tests of intellect over the years, particularly in the fact that neither of us has yet succeeded in stumping the other.

Admittedly, I have no guesses for how you managed to plant this logbook into my hands! You couldn't possibly have known that I would lift the possessions of a Kanjiklub chief engaged in negotiations for fiscal domination of the Rim territories.

But who else could this book be intended for, if not the Master Codebreaker?

Our private game of codes, ciphers, and cryptograms is like speaking a dead language. Only a few possess fluency, so holding a conversation is a rare delight.

Maz, I will solve your enigma, but I must build my legend in the meantime. Perfecting the arts of infiltration, espionage, and high-stakes bluffing requires that I rub extremities with the most valuable players in the galaxy.

With time and attention, they will all play my tune.

I have returned from the betting parlors of Hosnian Cardota, where I entertained a table of arms merchants while steadily whittling down their money supply. All of them could easily afford the loss, yet all took great offense when asked to slide over their chips. One eventually tried to poison me—the toxicity nullified by my hullepi-culture tongue sheath, of course—and I made my exit using a para-wing glider from the 350th-floor balcony.

The entire time, I found my attention drifting back to the mystery of this logbook.

I can't help but notice that your list of powerful crime syndicates is—of course—decades out of date. Furthermore, my experience in the Hosnian system made me realize that you neglected to credit the galaxy's true powers—perhaps by design?

MAZ'S LIST	SIGNIFICANT PLAYERS	CORPORATE ENTITIES
Black Sun	None (vigo diaspora)	Sienar Fleet Systems
Crymorah	Droid Gotra	BlasTech
Crimson Dawn	Son-Tuul Pride, Guavians	Kuat Drive Yards
Pykes	Kanjiklub/Red Key Raiders	Mining Guild
Hutts	Red Key Raiders/Kanjiklub	Corporate Sector Authority

I am certain these relationships conceal a clue. Applying a value (derived from resource control) to the first column and applying an exponential factor (from the second column's degree of sector domination) . . . renders a 16-integer security key of 8211002504757290.

No. If any data-drone could crack it, it is too simple a cipher-text.

I must take a break from puzzling to replenish my assets. I need credits, it's true, though I wouldn't say no to a well-mixed Chandrilan cocktail as well.

Until I return from the Brentaal trading houses, your cipher will have to wait. Brentaal is one of the few worlds that has not yet barred the Master Codebreaker from games involving the mental calculation of odds. It is certain to be a daredevilish outing.

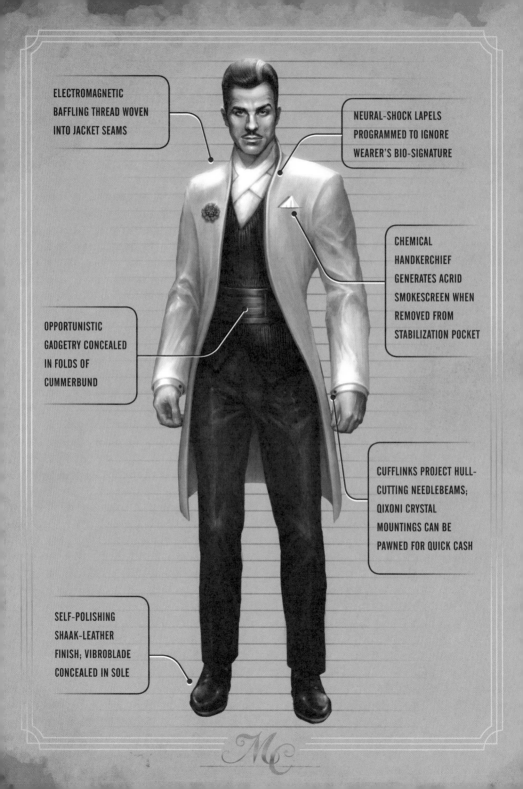

ELECTROMAGNETIC
BAFFLING THREAD WOVEN
INTO JACKET SEAMS

NEURAL-SHOCK LAPELS
PROGRAMMED TO IGNORE
WEARER'S BIO-SIGNATURE

CHEMICAL
HANDKERCHIEF
GENERATES ACRID
SMOKESCREEN WHEN
REMOVED FROM
STABILIZATION POCKET

OPPORTUNISTIC
GADGETRY CONCEALED
IN FOLDS OF
CUMMERBUND

CUFFLINKS PROJECT HULL-
CUTTING NEEDLEBEAMS;
QIXONI CRYSTAL
MOUNTINGS CAN BE
PAWNED FOR QUICK CASH

SELF-POLISHING
SHAAK-LEATHER
FINISH; VIBROBLADE
CONCEALED IN SOLE

Maz, you surely know that I released every scrap of my personal data on the public newsnets, masked only by a biohexacrypt code. Should any adversary obtain this information they are welcome to claim the mantle of Master Codebreaker.

It goes without saying that none have succeeded, and I realize that this may in itself be a clue. It was the Kupohans who developed the method of encoding information into organic genomes, and thus the textbook hexacrypt technique gained its "bio" prefix. An already thorny trail became all but impassable.

Take the simple plom bloom. Under biohexacrypt, each genetic strand acts as a scytale wrapped by a transposition cipher. Data rich and unpredictable.

I feel I could succeed in this line of inquiry if I could determine the biological sample you selected for encryption.

After my sojourn on Brentaal and parts spinward, I am reminded that very little ever really changes. Regardless of which faction holds power, business interests retain their grip on manufacturing. Republic or Empire, New Republic or First Order—everyone is in the market for the same merchandise.

Another thing that never changes is my choice of drink, and this is a fact you know well. Therefore, my intellectual adversary, I am digitizing this text into radial shells before applying a biohexacrypt key derived from the genome of the jogan fruit, my preferred cocktail garnish.

The results are back from my biohexacrypt key, and I have spent hours poring over them with an eye for your particular style of wit and wordplay.

I can only conclude that this logbook is an elaborate, living cipher. I have taken everything into account: the number of pages, the course of its interstellar journey, which treasures have been pursued and which have not, the count of years since creation plus the average time of possession for each owner, the density of words on each page, the degree of environmental wear, and countless additional factors. Whenever I wondered if I was overthinking it, I recalled your exceptional craftiness.

Biohexacrypt cracking didn't provide an immediate answer, but after manually scanning for patterns I saw it. Taking each seventy-second character with an exponential step factor applied at regular intervals renders the following:

$$H - A - [P] - P - [Y]$$

$$[F] - E - T - [E] \quad W - [E] - E - K$$

(The bracketed characters are speculative, but some data may have been lost during decryption.)

My dear Maz, is this entire logbook your way of wishing me a prosperous New Year Fete? I thank you, and extend the same to you in return.

———————|———————

Now, how might I match your subtlety by nudging this logbook so its course bends back to Takodana?

Perhaps I will place it inside the very YT-1300 freighter operated by several of your unwitting agents. The *Millennium Falcon*, isn't it?

Locating its owner is trivial, and placing this logbook on board is even easier. I doubt Solo will even realize it's there.

And so I send this book back to you, old friend. I hope I have solved your cryptogram, and if not I trust you are amused by my efforts.

As always, I remain, the Master Codebreaker.

P. S. Lovey sends her best.

Is this Solo's logbook? It's not the CEC one that comes with a factory-fresh YT freighter, but I wouldn't be surprised if he lost that one ages ago. This'll do for recording the acquisition of title.

Gannis Ducain

Solo should really keep a closer eye on his possessions!

Found this in the cockpit. An odd-looking logbook, but looks official or close enough.

The *Millennium Falcon* is now owned by the Irving Boys.

Toursant Irving

Vanver Irving

NIIMA OUTPOST, JAKKU
RESALE LOT AND CONCESSION STAND
UNKAR PLUTT, PROPRIETOR

ACQUIRED ASSET:

YT-1300 freighter *Millennium Falcon*

NOTES

Doesn't look like much on the outside. Could get some money by pushing the engines and the navicomputer. "This little number has got it where it counts!"

If nobody makes an offer, strip it for parts.

OPERATOR'S LICENSE

CEC BALEEN-CLASS HEAVY FREIGHTER

SHIP NAME

ERAVANA

WEAPONS LOADOUT

UNARMED

HYPERDRIVE

CLASS 2

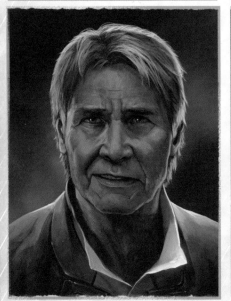

PRIMARY HOLDER

SOLO, HAN

SECONDARY HOLDER

CHEWBACCA

It ain't fair. I've got to get a new image taken every few years, but Chewie hasn't aged a day. To Wookiees, we humans are basically pets.

I told him that if he takes another life debt after I check out, I'm gonna come back and haunt him. That's something you can do with the Force, isn't it? —Han

I MUST BE SOME KIND OF BLACK HOLE for this thing to keep surfacing in my path like this, right? Any fortune-tellers want to explain why I'm seeing this bad omen again and again?

At least Chewie's happy about it. Keeps opening it up to different pages and laugh-snuffling. He says it's good luck this thing keeps coming back, but I know better.

If that were true, things would've turned out differently. Everything would be different. Honestly, what else could I have expected? What could a guy like me offer someone like her?

Skip the buried treasures and all that skuff. There's nothing wrong with going after the easy targets. Me and Chewie, we were doing okay running cargo on the *Eravana*. Almost got me feeling like I was young and dumb again.

That's when we ran into the *Millennium Falcon*. I've been walking her corridors ever since. The fresh smell of thread grease. That stale funk from the couch fabric. The way the aircycler makes that whine before it switches off. Chewie's giant feet clomping all over the hollow deck plates.

We're on our way to Takodana. I could easily drop this logbook off with Maz. But now I'm starting to feel like it's mine, and after getting the *Falcon* back I'm in no hurry to start giving away more stuff.

That girl, Rey. She'd be good to have aboard the *Falcon*. I could show her what I know. I'm not getting younger and having someone who can get down in the hatches would be good. And maybe she could carry on after I'm gone. Another roll of the dice. A scoundrel's redemption.

Regrets have gotta be the worst part of getting old. Can't stop thinking of things I said ages ago that maybe I shouldn't have said. I spent so many years trying to become the person I wanted to be that I eventually started pushing away those who were smart enough to see it was all an act. I should have been a better partner, and a better father.

What if I could do it all over again? Honestly, things would probably play out the same. Not much point in thinking about it, though. Constantly looking over your shoulder is a pretty good way to keep going in circles.

You can't change yesterday, so there's no use getting all sad about it. But tomorrow? Look out.

Oh, Han. You beautiful, intractable idiot.

Paging through this book is like meeting you all over again. The outlaw braggart. The reluctant rebel. You infuriated me, and you knew it.

How many times did I threaten to throw you out of the airlock, or dump you on a dead moon? But who other than a stubborn scoundrel like you could have pushed through my carefully crafted shields to reach the heartbroken orphan on the other side?

After Alderaan, I swore I'd never get close to anyone again. And then there you were, with your arrogance and that smirk and yes, I'll admit it, those tight pants. I never had a chance, did I?

I had you pegged the moment I laid eyes on you. An outlaw, a troublemaker, a reprobate. Did you know that they say you can learn a lot about a person by the company they keep? If this logbook is any indication, I was right all along.

I know what you'd say to that. You'd tell me that someone's character shouldn't be defined by their line of work. And I'd probably argue with you, out of habit, even though the proof of your words would be standing right there in front of me.

You spent a lifetime running away from your regrets, Han. I see that they started to weigh on you toward the end, and I wish I could talk to you one more time. I'd tell you that regrets aren't something to be ashamed of. They're a chance to step back and take stock of your life before moving forward once more. Regrets allow you to see with compassion, to understand that others have made your same mistakes.

I know you always wondered, and the answer is no. I never regretted our time together. I loved you, nerf herder. I still do.

The *Falcon*, she's Chewie's ship now. And Rey reminds me so much of you. Not a single credit to her name but she's got enough guts to take on the galaxy. I'm putting this logbook back into the *Falcon* where it will keep sailing on. It couldn't ask for better caretakers.

So long, flyboy. Force willing, we'll see each other again.

— Leia

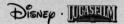

Library of Congress Cataloging-in-Publication Data available.

ISBN: 978-1-4521-8235-3

Smuggler's Guide: Tales From the Underworld was first published by Epic Ink, an Imprint of the Quarto Group
11120 NE 33rd Place, Suite 201
Bellevue, Washington 98004
www.QuartoKnows.com

Design: Sam Dawson
Editorial: Delia Greve
Production: Tom Miller

Manufactured in China

MIX
Paper from
responsible sources
FSC® C016973

Author: Daniel Wallace
Illustration: Adrián Rodriguez: pages 9, 10, 13, 16, 17, 19, 22, 30, 32-33, 35, 42, 44, 50, 74, 86-87, 88, 89, 91, 92, 93, 94, 104, 106, 107, 108, 113; Studio Hive: pages 8, 12, 14, 21, 23, 54, 57, 58, 61, 62, 63, 64, 69, 70, 77, 101, 110, 111, 112 (top), 115, 119, 125, 128, 131, 133, 134, 136, 142, 150, 156; Javier Charro: pages 38, 40, 66-67, 71, 81, 82-83, 112 (bottom), 120, 122, 124, 137, 138

Image credits (used throughout): 47236681 © Valentin Agapov/Shutterstock; 269387966 © Ataly/Shutterstock; 327470060 © howcolour/Shutterstock

10 9 8 7 6 5 4 3 2 1

Chronicle Books LLC
680 Second Street
San Francisco, California 94107

www.chroniclebooks.com